The Tale of Bushy the Fox

and

Other Stories

by
ENID BLYTON

Illustrated by
Val Biro

AWARD PUBLICATIONS LIMITED

For further information on Enid Blyton please visit *www.blyton.com*

ISBN 978-1-84135-479-8

This edition entitled *The Tale of Bushy the Fox and Other Stories*
published by permission of Chorion Rights Limited

This edition first published by Award Publications Limited 2006

Published by Award Publications Limited,
The Old Riding School, The Welbeck Estate,
Worksop, Nottinghamshire, S80 3LR

10 9 8 7 6 5 4 3 2
20 19 18 17 16 15 14 13 12 11 10 09 08

Printed in the United Kingdom

CONTENTS

The Tale of
Bushy the Fox

Bushy was a young fox. He lived with his father and mother and little brothers and sisters in a den under a big gorse bush on the common. But he wasn't at all happy there.

He wanted to go out and explore the world, but his mother wouldn't let him.

"Why can't I?" said Bushy, crossly. "The rabbits play over there on the hillside, and nobody tells them not to. The horse and the donkey are down there in the field and come to no harm. The dog barks down at the farmyard and I see him wandering about all over the place. Why can't I go where I like? I am as clever as anybody else."

"Oh, no you're not!" said his mother,

sharply. "It's only stupid foxes that want to leave their den before they are old enough. You must learn all kinds of things from me and your father before you are allowed out alone. You may be chased by hounds – what would you do then? You may find a farmer with a gun, and he will shoot you – what would you do then?"

"Oh, I daresay I should think of something," said the fox cub. "Anyway, I don't want to grow up to be a fox, if I'm going to be hunted like that. I'd rather be a dog, or a cat, or a horse or even a hen! Men keep all those things and feed them well. I don't want to be a fox."

"Well, let me tell you this – you couldn't do any of the things that those creatures are clever enough to do," said his mother, cuffing him. "You think you are clever, don't you, Master Bushy? – but you're not!"

Bushy was angry when his mother cuffed him. He went right to the back of the den and thought and thought.

"When nobody is looking tonight, I

will slip out of the hole and go to seek my fortune," he thought. "I will visit the dog and the cat, the horse and the hen, and I will see if I can grow up into something else instead of a fox!"

So that night, when his father and mother were out hunting for food, and his brothers and sisters lay all curled up in a heap, fast asleep, Bushy crept out of the den. He scampered down the hillside to the farm.

The first creature he saw was old Captain, the brown-and-white horse. He was standing under a tree, half asleep. Bushy made him jump when he spoke to him.

"Excuse me, big horse, but will you

7

please tell me if it's easy to be a horse?" asked Bushy, politely.

Captain tried to see who was talking to him, but he couldn't.

"Oh, it's quite easy," he said. "You have to be able to do a few things, of course."

"What do you have to do?" asked Bushy.

"Oh, nothing much," said Captain. "You must be able to pull a cart, to plough a field, to carry a rider. You must wear a saddle and bridle, you must know which way to go when your master twitches the reins, you must—"

"Oh dear!" said Bushy in dismay. "I should never be able to do all that! Good evening to you. I shan't be a horse."

The next creature he saw was the cat, Mouser. She was lying down on a mat outside the farmhouse door. She couldn't see Bushy, but she answered him when he spoke.

"Excuse me, cat, but will you please tell me if it's easy to be a cat?" asked Bushy.

"Oh, it's quite easy," said Mouser. "You

have to be able to do a few things, of course."

"What do you have to do?" asked Bushy.

"Oh, nothing much," said Mouser. "You must be able to catch all the mice, and fight the rats – and they can bite very fiercely! You must be able to mew when you are hungry, and purr when you are pleased. You must—"

"Oh my!" said Bushy. "I could never mew or purr, I know! And I'm afraid of rats, just at present. Good evening to you. I shan't be a cat!"

He went on his way once more, and soon came to the hen-house. One hen was awake, and Bushy spoke to her through the wire netting. She couldn't see him, or she might have been frightened.

"Excuse me, hen, but will you please tell me if it's easy to be a hen?" he asked, politely.

"Oh, it's quite easy," said the hen. "You have to be able to lay eggs, of course, and cackle loudly when you've laid them.

You have to be able to bring up chicks, and cluck, and you must always obey the cockerel."

"Well, I could never obey a silly old cockerel!" said Bushy. "And I couldn't ever lay an egg, I'm sure. Good evening to you. I shan't be a hen!"

Very soon he came to where a large pig lay in a sty.

"Excuse me, pig," said Bushy, "but will you please tell me if it's easy to be a pig?"

"Very easy," said the pig, grunting, "and it's easier still to be bacon! I'll change places with you, if you like. You can live a lazy life here in my sty and be made into bacon in the autumn, and I'll run about free and live my life in the open!"

"Oh my, I never want to be bacon!" said the fox cub, shivering. "Good evening to you. I shan't be a pig!"

Off he went again, and came to the dog's kennel. Pincher, the sheepdog, was wide awake, and he sniffed at Bushy as he came near.

"Excuse me, dog, but will you please tell me if it's easy to be a dog?" Bushy asked politely.

"Oh, it's quite easy," said Pincher. "You have to be able to do a few things, of course."

"What do you have to do?" asked Bushy.

"Well, you must be able to look after sheep, and see that those clever foxes don't take the lambs," said Pincher. "You must be able to guard the farmyard and see that no fox steals the hens. You must look after the young ducks, for those sly foxes are always after them. You must be able to bark at foxes, and seize them – like this!"

Pincher suddenly leaped at Bushy, and very nearly caught him. The frightened cub jumped away just in time. Pincher began to snarl and growl.

"I know you're a fox!" he snapped. "What do you mean by coming into my farmyard and asking foolish questions? Whoever heard of a fox wanting to be any other animal! Why, foxes are the cleverest creatures in the countryside! Wuff! Wuff-wuff!"

Pincher began to bark loudly, and the farmer threw up his window and leaned out. The ducks quacked, the hens clucked, the pig grunted. What a fearful noise there was!

Bushy was glad to slink out of the farmyard unseen. He raced back to his den on the hillside and was very happy to be curled up among his brothers and sisters once more.

"How foolish I am to want to be some other creature, not a fox," he thought. "Why, no other animal is so clever! Who wants to drag a plough, to lay an egg, to mew and purr, or to look after hens and ducks? No, I will catch hens and ducks, I will make that barking dog afraid of me. I want to be a fox and nothing else!"

How surprised Bushy's mother was next day to find what an obedient little cub Bushy was. She didn't know he had been out all night, talking to the farmyard creatures – and Bushy didn't tell her, because he knew she would cuff him!

The Very
Strange Hat

There was once an old woman called Mother Clumps. She lived in a tiny cottage all by herself, for she hadn't even a cat. She was a most disagreeable old woman, with a turned-down mouth, two sharp eyes and a big thick stick that she always took with her when she went out.

The children were afraid of her. The grown-ups didn't like her. The dogs kept away from her because of her big stick. So, as you can guess, she had no friends at all, and she wasn't very happy.

Now, though she was disagreeable, she wanted a friend that she could sometimes ask in to tea. She often wished that old Dame Clutter would smile at her and say good morning. "Then," thought

Mother Clumps, "I would smile back and say 'Come in and have a cup of tea.'"

Or perhaps if Old Man Tiptap would just raise his cap to her and nod, she would nod back and say "Come along and taste my new scones." But nobody ever did smile or say good morning or even nod. And it wasn't any wonder either, for Mother Clumps always looked so dreadfully disagreeable that nobody dared to pass the time of day with her. Most people didn't even look at the cross old woman. They knew her quite well, for she always went out shopping each

morning, her old red shawl round her shoulders and her warm woollen hat pulled tightly down on her head to keep out the wind.

Now, one morning Mother Clumps woke up feeling really very lonely indeed. She had made a most wonderful gingerbread cake the day before – so delicious that she simply longed for someone to taste it and say how lovely it was. She lay in bed and wondered why she had no friends. Why were people so horrid?

The sun came in at the window. It was a beautiful day. Mother Clumps could smell the roses peeping in at the window. Oh, if only someone would smile at her or just give her a nod! The foolish old woman didn't once think that if only she would smile and nod herself it would make all the difference! No, she just lay and thought that really, people were most disagreeable and unkind.

She got up and dressed. She ate her breakfast and took another look at her beautiful gingerbread cake. Dear me, it really was perfect! Such a lovely colour! So sweet! So spicy on the tongue! What a pity there was no one to admire it.

"Well, I suppose I must go and do my shopping," thought Mother Clumps, getting up in a hurry from the table. Her sleeve caught the teapot handle and over it went, spilling the dregs of the brown tea on the nice clean red tablecloth!

"Bother!" said Mother Clumps, crossly. "Look at that now! Clean on today, too!"

She cleared the table and then soaked the stained part of the cloth in water. She laid the tablecloth over a chair to dry. The woollen tea-cosy had got a little stained too, so she dabbed that with water and put it beside the cloth to dry as well.

Then she went to wash up. Outside the birds were singing loudly. The sun streamed in at the kitchen window and made old Mother Clumps blink, it was so bright.

"That sun will fade my blue carpet!" she said. "I'll draw down the blind." So she pulled down the blind and darkened

the kitchen to save her carpet, which
was a very pretty blue. Then off she went
to dust the parlour.

After that it was time to go out. "I
must hurry up and do my shopping or all
the best things will be gone!" said the
old woman. "I'll put on my red shawl
and hat. Now where are they? In the
kitchen? Yes, I think I saw them there."

She went to the kitchen, which was
still dark with the drawn blind. She saw
a big red thing hanging over the back of

a chair, and a small woolly thing beside it. "Good!" she said. "Here they are!"

But, you know, it wasn't her shawl she saw, and it wasn't her hat! It was her red tablecloth she had hung over the chair to dry, and the woollen tea-cosy beside it! In the dim light the old dame quite thought they were hat and shawl, so she picked up the tablecloth and flung it round her shoulders. And then she picked up the woollen tea-cosy, with its funny little tassel at the top, and crammed that down over her head. Dear me, she did look funny with a tablecloth round her and a tea-cosy on her head!

She took up her shopping basket and out she went, her big stick going *tap-tap-tap* down the path. What a lovely day it was! Old Mother Clumps felt quite happy to see such golden sunshine all around.

"If only someone would smile at me today!" she thought. "But they're a disagreeable lot, the people in this village!"

But someone did smile at her – the very first person she met! It was Old

Man Tiptap – and, you know, he really could not help smiling when he saw Mother Clumps coming along in a tea-cosy and a tablecloth. She did look so very funny. He didn't dare to tell her what she had got on, for she always looked so extremely disagreeable, but really, really, he could not for the life of him stop a smile coming to his mouth at the sight of the old dame!

Mother Clumps saw him smiling and she was simply delighted. Here was someone smiling at her at last! Oh, how nice it made her feel! She smiled too and called to the old man.

"Good morning, Old Man Tiptap! Come along and taste my new gingerbread cake this afternoon, will you?"

Old Man Tiptap was so astonished to see Mother Clumps smile and to hear her invitation that he could hardly answer at first. Then he nodded his head, and said "Very pleased, I'm sure!" Then still smiling broadly he hurried on his way.

The next people the old dame met were the three small children of Mrs Biscuit, the baker. Usually they ran away when they saw Mother Clumps, but today they were so astonished to see her in a tea-cosy and a tablecloth that they stood laughing all over their little rosy faces as she came along. They did not call out, for they had good manners, but they couldn't help smiling.

"More smiles for me today!" thought old Mother Clumps, in delight. "Dear little children! I'll give them a silver penny each!"

The children could not believe their eyes when the old dame gave them each a silver penny. She had never given anyone anything before.

"Oh thank you, you are kind!" said the children, and they beamed all over their little fat faces.

Mother Clumps felt a sudden warm feeling inside her when she saw them so delighted. It was lovely.

"Come along this afternoon to my cottage and bring your mother," she said. "I've a wonderful new gingerbread cake you'll like to taste!"

The children ran off, excited. They kept turning back to see the old dame in her tea-cosy and tablecloth. She turned back too and waved. So they waved back.

"Really!" thought Mother Clumps, very happily. "I'd no idea that children could be so sweet."

Soon she met Dame Clutter, also going shopping. Dame Clutter stared in amazement when she saw what Mother Clumps was wearing. She turned her head away to hide her smiles – but Mother Clumps saw her smiling and called out eagerly, "Good morning, Dame Clutter! A fine day, isn't it? Do come along this afternoon and have a piece of my new gingerbread cake!"

Dame Clutter was so astonished to see the happy look on Mother Clumps's face and to hear her invitation that she stared in surprise. Then she smiled again and said yes, she would be pleased to come that afternoon. She hurried on her way, thinking what a strange thing it was that Mother Clumps should wear a tea-cosy and a tablecloth and suddenly seem so much nicer and quite friendly. Whatever had come over her?

Mother Clumps went on, feeling happy and pleased. All the children she met laughed or smiled, and she gave away all her money. She liked the nice warm feeling it gave her to see the children's

surprise and delight. She nodded to Mr
Steak, the butcher, who beamed all over
his red face when he saw the old dame so
strangely dressed, and she asked him to
share her cake that afternoon too.

"I've never known everyone so friendly
and nice before!" thought Mother
Clumps. "Never! Why, they seem
different people! Perhaps they have found
out that I am quite a nice person really,
so they want to be friends. Just look at
the way they smile when they meet me!
I haven't met a single person yet that
hasn't smiled as soon as they caught
sight of me!"

Mother Clumps got home at twelve
o'clock. The sun was no longer shining
into the kitchen so she pulled up the
blind as soon as she got in. She
remembered how she had spilt the tea at
breakfast-time on her tablecloth and tea-
cosy and she looked round for them to
put them away. But she couldn't see
them anywhere! They simply weren't
there! How strange!

And then – oh dear me – Mother

Clumps suddenly saw her red shawl and her woollen hat on the chest by the wall! She stared at them as if she couldn't believe her eyes.

"My shawl!" she said. "And my hat! But I've got them on. I've worn them all the morning. How could they be on me and on the chest too?"

She went over to the big looking-glass and stared at herself – and then she saw what she had been wearing all the morning – her big old woollen tea-cosy with the tassel sticking up at the top, and her red tablecloth!

She stared and stared at herself. How funny she looked! How could she have gone out like that? How dreadful! Her eyes suddenly filled with tears. Oh dear! Oh dear!

She sat down and thought.

"So that's why people smiled at me – because I looked so funny! No wonder they laughed all over their faces! No wonder the children stood and stared – and I thought everyone was so friendly. I was so happy, so pleased. And I've asked about twelve people to tea this afternoon!"

She took off the tea-cosy and threw it into a corner. She slipped off the tablecloth and flung it over a chair. She frowned and pouted – and then she caught sight of herself in the glass.

"Good gracious!" said the old woman,

in horror. "Do I really look as disagreeable as all that? No wonder nobody wants to know me! Dear, dear me, Mother Clumps, let this be a lesson to you! You thought everyone so nice this morning because they smiled and looked pleasant – so just you do the same! Smile now!"

She smiled at herself in the glass and then looked most astonished.

"Well I never!" she said. "Who would have thought I looked so nice when I smiled? My eyes twinkle and my cheeks

screw up in the nicest way! I'd better smile more often. I'm quite nice-looking when I do!"

Then she sat and thought about all the invitations she had given to tea. What should she do? She went quite red when she thought of how people must have laughed at her that morning. But they had all been polite and nice, and very well-mannered.

"I'll have them all to tea as I said!" cried Mother Clumps, jumping up in excitement. "I'm not going to be a disagreeable old woman any more! This is a great chance for me and I'll never have one like it again. I'm going straight out to buy some chocolate biscuits, some strawberry jam, some thick cream and a jam sandwich. I'm going to make some scones too, and, with the gingerbread cake, that will be a fine tea!"

Off she rushed once more, this time with her own hat on and her proper shawl. She bought all the things she wanted and then she stopped and looked at a draper's shop. In it was a fine black

silk dress, a beautiful blue shawl and the
sweetest little white lace cap that anyone
could wish for.

"I'll buy those too!" said Mother
Clumps, in excitement. "If I'm going to
be a nice, friendly old woman I'll want to
look nice. I'm tired of my old things. I'll
soon make people forget that I went out
today dressed in my tea-cosy and
tablecloth!"

So she bought the dress, the fine shawl

and the lace cap. She hurried home, and goodness me, wasn't she busy for the rest of the day! When four o'clock came and her twelve visitors came knocking at the door, what a sight met their eyes!

Instead of a dingy kitchen, a table set with a few cakes, and a cross-looking old dame in a dirty red shawl, they saw a bright kitchen with a table loaded with good things, and a bowl of shining marigolds in the middle. They stared at Mother Clumps in surprise too – for they saw a pretty old lady, smiling all over her face, dressed in a soft black dress, with a lovely blue shawl across her shoulders and a pretty lace cap on her hair. Could this be Mother Clumps, the cross old dame that everyone disliked and was afraid of?

What a fine time everyone had! How they ate and drank, how they talked and laughed! They all said that the gingerbread cake was the finest they had ever eaten – and do you know there wasn't even a crumb of it left! Mother Clumps was so proud and pleased.

"Come to tea with me tomorrow!" said Dame Clutter.

"And with me on Friday!" said Old Man Tiptap.

"And with us on Saturday!" cried the baker's children.

Nobody said a word about how they had seen Mother Clumps that morning looking so funny in the cosy and cloth. Wasn't it kind of them? After they had all gone, Mother Clumps cleared away very happily. There was a lot of washing-up to do, but what did she care? Such nice friends were worth a bit of extra work, yes, indeed they were!

Now Mother Clumps is one of the best-liked people in the village – and isn't it strange to think that it all came about because she went out shopping in a tea-cosy and a tablecloth? Well, well, you never know what's going to happen to you in this world!

A Surprise for Molly

The children were in the playroom, playing with their toys, when their mother called to them.

"Alan! Molly! You really must go out into the garden this nice sunny day! Hurry now!"

"Oh, Mummy – just a minute!" cried Molly. "I'm putting my doll to bed. She's got measles."

"Well, it would be better to take her out in her pram on a nice day like this," said Mother, coming into the playroom.

"Mummy, it would be dangerous," said Molly. "Alan's the doctor, and he told me to keep Angela in bed for two days. Please just let me finish tucking her up."

"Very well," said Mother. "Then go out and play till I call you in for lunch. And come in with good appetites, please, because there will be egg salad. There will be juicy little tomatoes and cucumber too, so come in as soon as you hear me call."

Molly finished putting her doll to bed. Angela's bed was a big cardboard box that her mother had lined for her with some pink padded silk. Mother had made her a pillow too, and Molly herself had made the little sheets and blankets. Angela really looked sweet in the bed.

"Hurry up," said Alan, impatiently. "I want to play Indians!"

"I'm ready now," said Molly, and she stood up. "Goodbye, Angela dear. I hope you will go to sleep."

The two children went out into the sunny garden. It was lovely out there. The sun was warm, the bees were humming, and the sparrows were chirping madly.

"Now we're Indians," said Alan. "Here's a spear for you. We'll hide in the bushes and jump out if an enemy comes."

It took them all the morning to play their game, and they were hot, hungry and tired at the end of it. They were pleased to hear their mother call them in for lunch.

"Good!" said Alan. "Egg salad – cucumber – lettuce, and radishes, I expect – and little juicy tomatoes out of the greenhouse. Hurrah!"

They ran in. Mother called to them from the playroom, where she was busy setting out the lunch. "Wash your hands and brush your hair, please."

They were always supposed to do that before a meal, but they always had to be told. Off they went to wash, and then they brushed their hair neatly.

There came a ring at the front door bell just then. Mother had to go and see who it was, and then spend a few minutes talking to the caller. The children were impatient because they were hungry. They waited in the hall for their mother. At last she shut the front door and came over to them.

"Well, I'm ready at last," she said. "Come along."

They went into the playroom. Mother had set the lunch out on the table by the window. Alan ran over to it. He looked at the salad.

"Oh, Mum! You said we would have cucumber but there isn't a single bit on the dish! And there aren't any tomatoes either."

"Yes, there are," said Mother. "I put them there myself!"

But when she came over to the table, too, she stared in surprise. Alan was quite right. There wasn't any cucumber, and not a single tomato either!

Mother turned the salad over with a spoon. No – there really was only lettuce and radishes. How very strange! She looked at the two children.

"You haven't slipped in here, surely, and eaten the cucumber and tomatoes yourselves?" she asked.

"Of course not, Mummy!" cried both children at once. "You know we wouldn't."

Their mother looked all round the playroom as if to see who would possibly have taken some of the salad. "It's most extraordinary," she said. "No bird would come and steal the cucumber and tomatoes – and certainly no cat or dog

40

would. Then who in the world has taken them?"

Alan and Molly looked all round the playroom, too, but they couldn't see anyone or anything that might have stolen their salad. Then Molly suddenly noticed something that made her cry out in surprise.

"Who's thrown Angela out of her bed? Look – poor darling, she's lying on the floor, face downwards – and she's ill with the measles, too. Alan – did you do that?"

"No, I didn't," said Alan. "Of course I didn't. Aren't I Angela's doctor? Would I throw a patient out of her bed on to the floor? Don't be silly."

"Well, who did, then?" cried Molly. She ran over to her doll and picked her up.

"Molly, you really must come and have lunch now," said Mother, thinking that Molly would be a long time tucking her doll up in bed again. "Come along now. You can see to Angela afterwards."

"Oh, Mummy, just let me put her into bed," said Molly. She put her hand on the little blankets to pull them back – and then she gave such a squeal that Mother and Alan almost jumped out of their seats.

"Ooo! There's somebody in my doll's bed! Look! Look! What is it?"

Mother and Alan ran to see. And whatever do you suppose was lying fast asleep in the little bed? You would never, never guess, I'm sure! It was a small brown monkey, curled up under the sheets, his head on the pillow, fast asleep!

"Is he real?" said Alan. "Yes – he must

42

be. He's breathing. Oh, Molly, I do think he's rather sweet."

"Why – he must be Major Beeton's pet monkey!" cried Mother, in surprise. "I met him this morning, and he told me the little thing had escaped. You know, he is usually kept in a big cage, and he has a little basket in the cage with a pillow and blankets that he rolls himself in. That's why he has cuddled down into your doll's bed, Molly. It reminded him of his own little basket."

"Well, he shouldn't have thrown poor Angela out," said Molly. "Mummy, doesn't he look funny in my doll's bed?"

"Mummy, was it the monkey who took our cucumber and tomatoes from the salad?" asked Alan, suddenly. "Do monkeys like them?"

"Of course!" said Mother. "He must have looked in at the window and seen our nice lunch on the table and he just helped himself to what he liked the most! Then he wanted to sleep, and found himself a bed."

"I like him," said Alan. "I wish we could keep him. If Molly didn't want him to sleep in her doll's bed I would let him have my big bicycle basket."

"I expect Major Beeton will want him back," said Mother. "Shut the window, will you, Alan. And you shut the door, Molly. Then if he wakes he can't get out. I'll go and telephone Major Beeton."

Mother went off to the phone. The children shut the door and the window. Their mother soon came back. "Major Beeton is delighted that we have found Marmaduke," she said.

"Oh, is that his name?" asked Alan.

"Doesn't it suit him. Marmaduke the monkey. It's lovely."

Marmaduke woke up when he heard his name. He sat up in bed and looked at the children and their mother. Then he jumped out, ran to the table and climbed up on Molly's knee. She was so pleased that she could hardly speak.

"Oh, I wish we could keep him," she said. "I do like him so. I love my dolls and my other toys – but they don't run about and climb on my knee like Marmaduke."

Marmaduke behaved himself very well indeed. He took a bit of lettuce from Molly's plate and nibbled a bit of hard-boiled egg that Alan gave him. He loved the ripe plum that Mother took from the dish on the dresser, and the children thought he was very clever when he carefully took off the skin before eating it. He was rather rude about the stone, though. He spat it out on the floor.

"He ought to belong to us, really," said Alan, picking up the stone. "We could teach him his manners."

When Major Beeton came to get his monkey the children were sad. "We do wish we could have him," said Molly. "You know, Major Beeton, he hasn't got very beautiful manners – but I'm sure he could learn."

"Well, you come and teach him some, then," said Major Beeton. "Come to tea with me each week, and we'll have old Marmaduke out of his cage. You shall play with him and teach him as many manners as you like. But I'm not sure he'll learn them!"

The children were simply delighted. They are going to tea with Marmaduke tomorrow – and what do you think Molly has got as a present for him? A little pillow for his bed. Won't Marmaduke like that!

Tinker-dog
and Prince

Tinker-dog lived with his master in a little tumbledown cottage at the end of Tiptop Village. He wasn't a terrier, and he wasn't a collie, and he wasn't an Alsatian. I couldn't tell you what he was – he just wasn't anything but a plain dog. But his master loved him and called him a fine fellow.

Prince was a beautiful Alsatian dog, so like a grand wolf that you could hardly tell he wasn't. He was worth a lot of money, and he was as proud as could be. He walked along the road as if it belonged to him, and if he met Tinker-dog he growled at him angrily.

"Growl away, Prince High and Mighty!" Tinker barked back. "I can race you any day, though you run like the

48

wind! My legs are as good as yours!"

"Common little dog!" said Prince, in his deep, growly voice. "Keep out of my way. I am a prize dog. I win prizes at shows. You wouldn't win a prize at all – except for the ugliest, commonest dog in the show. Woooooooof!"

Tinker-dog ran home. He was sometimes a bit sad because he knew quite well he was a common little dog, and would certainly never win a prize at any show. He didn't want a prize for himself – but it would be so nice to win a prize for his master, whom he loved very much!

Now one day Prince and Tinker met by the river. "Woooooooof!" said Prince, snarling at Tinker-dog. "Why don't you keep out of my way? I don't like your looks. I don't like your smell. I don't like your—"

"I don't like your manners!" said Tinker, and he actually bit the end of Prince's tail! What would have happened next I don't know – but, just at that moment, a little boy who was playing by the river suddenly gave a scream and fell right into the water!

"Help! Help!" shouted the other children. Prince stared at the water. Tinker-dog stared too and barked to Prince: "You are a big strong dog. Jump in and pull the little boy out!"

But Prince ran away! It was Tinker-dog who jumped into the cold water and swam bravely to the little boy. He caught hold of the child's coat and then turned back to the bank. How heavy the little boy was! Tinker-dog puffed and panted, but he didn't let go! He struggled on and on.

"Look at that good little dog!" suddenly cried a man's voice. "He's got the child safely! Come on – let's help him!"

But Tinker needed no help. Just at that moment he reached the bank, and the little boy, spluttering and choking, climbed out, pulled by the other children.

"Brave dog! Good dog!" cried all the watching people, for there was now quite a crowd by the river. "Who is he? Why, he is the little dog belonging to Mr Brown!"

Tinker-dog didn't know what all the fuss was about. He shook himself well and ran off home.

"Brave dog! Good dog!" everyone shouted after him. And then someone said, "I saw that great big Alsatian dog called Prince run away! He didn't rescue Tommy! He was a coward – he ran away and left the job to a dog three times as small as himself! Tinker-dog deserves a medal!"

Soon the news about Tinker-dog was all round the town! A newspaper man came to see Tinker-dog's master and took Tinker's photograph! It was in the paper next morning and underneath Tinker's picture it said:

"The finest dog in our town. Tinker-dog, who saved little Tommy from the river! What shall we give him for a reward?"

Now the next week there was a dog

52

show in the town, and, of course, Prince was going, for he hoped to win the best prizes. And do you know, a man came to Tinker-dog's master and asked him to take Tinker too.

"He won't win a prize for being a beautiful dog," he said, "but the dog-show people want to give him a medal and a fine red collar because he is the bravest dog they know. Little Tommy is to give it to him!"

So Tinker-dog, much to his surprise, was taken to the show, nicely washed and brushed. Prince went too – and when he saw Tinker-dog he laughed and said, "Fancy you turning up at my show, Tinker! Coming to see me take all the prizes?"

"Hello, funny-face!" said Tinker-dog, and ran along beside his master.

Prince did win a prize – but, oh dear, what do you suppose he felt like, when, at the end of the show, he saw the chief judge go up on to the platform and call for Tinker-dog.

"Now we come to the most important dog in the town!" said the judge, patting Tinker, who wagged his tail and looked most surprised. "This is Tinker-dog, who saved little Tommy from drowning last week. Prince, the big, prize-winning Alsatian, was by the river too – but he ran away! It was little Tinker-dog that jumped into the water! Three cheers for Tinker-dog!"

"Hip-hip-hip-hurrah!" shouted everyone. And then, up to the platform walked little Tommy, carrying a fine red collar with a silver medal hanging from it!

He put the collar round Tinker's neck.

How the medal shone and glittered when Tinker wagged his stumpy tail! He was the happiest dog in the world. His master was sitting nearby, looking so pleased, and proud of his dog. Tinker wuffed to him. "I've won a prize for you, master! I may be a common little dog, but I've done something after all!"

Everyone went home talking of Tinker-dog. Prince went home too, his tail drooping. What did it matter winning a prize for being splendid and beautiful to look at? Nobody looked at him – they all wanted to see Tinker, that common little dog! Prince sat by the fire and thought and thought.

"It isn't good looks that matter after all, or even good manners!" he thought to himself. "It is good deeds. I must tell Tinker when I see him."

So the next time he saw Tinker he ran over to him. "Tinker-dog, I may be a grand-looking dog, but you are a better dog than I am," he said. "I'd like to be friends with you, if you'll let me."

"Wuff-wuff! Of course," said Tinker. "Pleased to go for a walk with you any day, Prince!"

And now the two are always seen together, and perhaps one day Prince will be able to show that he can be as brave as Tinker. What do you think?

Mother Winkyn's Washing

There was once an old dame called Mother Winkyn, who lived all alone with her black cat in a cottage. She was a grumpy old thing, and never had a smile or a kind word for any boy or girl. As for giving any of them a penny, she never so much as thought of it.

"Boys and girls are just a nuisance," she would grumble to herself. "Noisy, shouting creatures! I don't like them. They're rude and selfish."

Well, of course, you couldn't expect any boy or girl to like Mother Winkyn either. None of them offered to run errands for her, and not one of them said good morning or smiled at her, for they were really quite afraid of her.

Now one morning Mother Winkyn did

her washing and pegged it out on the line. It was a very windy morning so she knew it would dry nice and quickly.

"I'll just put on my bonnet and go to do my shopping while my washing dries," said Mother Winkyn. So off she went with her basket, and left her line of washing dancing madly in the March wind.

No sooner had she turned the corner than the wind swooped down on the washing once again and began to tug at Mother Winkyn's best yellow petticoat, the one she wore under her Sunday dress. This petticoat was pegged up in the middle of the line of washing, and Mother Winkyn was very proud of it.

The wind tugged and tugged at it, and at last the petticoat flew from the pegs that held it and went sailing down the street. The boys and girls playing there saw it, and called out in delight.

"There goes Mother Winkyn's washing! Oh look! There goes Mother Winkyn's washing!"

One little boy looked rather worried.

"I say!" he said. "Oughtn't we to go after it? It will get lost. My mother was very worried once when my pyjamas blew away and were lost."

"Pooh! Let Mother Winkyn's washing get lost!" cried the other children. "Horrid old thing!"

"All the same, I don't like to see things blown away like that," said the little boy, watching the petticoat dance away down the street. "I think I'll go after it."

So off he went, the kind-hearted fellow, and tried to catch up with it. But as soon as he got near it the wind picked it up and blew it just a little further. It flew over the hedge and into a field. It landed on a cow and frightened it so much that it galloped round the field with the yellow petticoat hanging on its horns.

Then the petticoat dropped off, and the little boy ran to pick it up. Puff! The wind swept down again and off went the petticoat over the stream nearby to the field on the other side.

"Bother it!" said the little boy, quite determined now to get that petticoat somehow. He found a narrow place and jumped across the stream. Then he ran to get the yellow petticoat which was still lying in a flat heap on the grass. Puff! The wind blew down again and the petticoat danced off once more!

This time it flew towards the lane that led to the shops. On it went and the little boy ran after it. It sailed over a fence and into the lane. Then it danced round the corner where the baker's shop was.

The little boy raced after it. He rushed
round the corner and bumped straight
into someone, knocking her over and
sending her basket flying!

"Oh, bother you, you clumsy, careless
creature!" cried a cross voice. "Look what
you've done!"

The little boy looked. He was sorry
that he had knocked somebody down –
and dear me, who do you think it was? It
was Mother Winkyn coming back from

her shopping with her basket of potatoes and apples! They were spilt all over the road.

"Now you just pick them all up for me," scolded Mother Winkyn. "And then you come along with me and I'll complain to your mother how you rush about and knock people over, you horrid, rough child!"

The little boy was frightened. He picked up all the apples and potatoes and put them into the basket. Then he looked round for the petticoat. Ah, there it was, huddling in the doorway of the baker's shop. He rushed to it and caught it before the wind could send it flying into the air again. He bundled it under his arm and went back to Mother Winkyn, meaning to give it to her. But she had thought he was going to run off and she was cross.

"You hear what I say!" she scolded. "I'm going to make you come back with me and I'll tell your mother what a badly-behaved child you are. Throw that yellow rag down. What do you want to pick up rags for?"

"It isn't a rag, Mother Winkyn," said the little boy, "it's your petticoat."

Mother Winkyn stared at the yellow petticoat in surprise. Yes – it was her best Sunday petticoat. But how did it get here? She had left it on the washing-line!

"You see," explained the little boy, trotting by her side, "I was playing in the road outside and I saw the wind blow your petticoat away. So I went after it, because I know my mother gets upset when she loses anything. It blew such a long way away – and every time I got up to it the wind blew it away again. That's how I bumped into you round the corner. The petticoat had just blown round the corner, and I was afraid that if I didn't run hard I would lose it. I'm really very sorry I knocked you over."

Well! Mother Winkyn really didn't know what to say! She did wish she hadn't shouted at the little boy loudly. After all, he was only trying to get back some of her blown-away washing for her. He hadn't really meant to knock her over.

She looked down at the little boy. He was very much out of breath with all his running and his face was very rosy. He really looked a very nice little boy indeed – a very kind little boy. It was so nice of him to run after her washing like that – her very best yellow petticoat too. She wouldn't like to lose that.

Suddenly Mother Winkyn felt ashamed of herself. "You're a nice little fellow, and I'm sorry I scolded you," she said. "Of course I won't complain to your mother. I'll tell her you're the nicest little boy I know, instead. And perhaps one day you'd come to tea with me and we'll have chocolate cake and sugar biscuits."

Well, what do you think of that? The little boy couldn't believe his ears! But it was all quite true, and the very next day he went to tea with Mother Winkyn (his mother went too) and had the loveliest tea he had ever had in his life.

And now Mother Winkyn is quite changed. She smiles at all the children she meets and gives pennies to the ones she likes the best. She has a little tea-party every week and makes chocolate cake and sugar biscuits each time. The children like her very much and have quite forgotten she wasn't always like that!

Wasn't it a good thing that the little boy was kind enough to run after the washing that blew off the line? You never know what a kind deed will lead to, do you?

Now Then,
Mr Stamp-About

Mr Stamp-About was exactly like his name. He kept losing his temper, and then how he stamped about and bellowed and roared. It was dreadful to hear him.

Now, next door to him lived Pinky the pixie, and Pinky was really very much afraid of Mr Stamp-About. His cottage was joined to his neighbour's, and when Mr Stamp-About lost his temper, so that the cottages shook and shivered with his shouting and stamping, Pinky shook and shivered, too.

The worst of it was that Pinky never dared to go and ask Mr Stamp-About if he might get anything that fell in his garden. Sometimes Pinky's ball flew over – but did Pinky dare to ask for it back? Of course not.

"There must be at least five balls now that have fallen into Mr Stamp-About's garden," said Pinky mournfully. "And there's that aeroplane, too, which I made all by myself to fly high in the air. That went into his garden, too – but I'll never get it back!"

Once he did timidly ask Mr Stamp-About if he might get his things from the garden. Mr Stamp-About stared at him in angry surprise. "What! Let you come and trample all my garden down, looking for your silly balls and aeroplane?" he said. "You really must be mad!"

"Well, will you get them for me then?" asked Pinky.

"Oh, I'll get them all right – but not for you!" said Mr Stamp-About, with a nasty smile. And what do you think he did? Why, he went into his garden and found all five balls and the aeroplane, too – and he took them into his own house and kept them for himself!

"I've put them into my kitchen cupboard," he told Pinky. "And one of these days, when Pip the pedlar comes round, I'll sell them all to him. That will teach you not to throw things into my garden!"

After that, Pinky was really very careful. But he simply couldn't help the wind taking some of his arrows into Mr Stamp-About's garden when he was using his bow.

"Look at that now," said Pinky, climbing up on the wall with his bow. "Four out of my five arrows have fallen into Mr Stamp-About's garden. And I simply daren't get them."

He saw Mr Stamp-About shaking his

fist at him from the window. He called to him. "Hey, Mr Stamp-About, sir! Could you get me my four arrows? I'm sorry to say that the wind blew them into your garden."

Mr Stamp-About came stamping out. He picked up the four arrows – and then he stalked off indoors.

"Into my kitchen cupboard they'll go!" he shouted.

"You horrid thing!" cried Pinky, and he threw his bow angrily into Mr Stamp-About's garden, too. "What use is a bow without arrows? Take this, too!"

And will you believe it, Mr Stamp-About walked back, picked up the bow, and took that off as well! Pinky cried with anger and disappointment.

For a long time he was very careful. Then there came a day when he did a lot of washing. "I really must wash out my blankets," he said. "And there are my curtains, too – and those cushion covers. It's a nice day for drying things, so I'll do all my washing today."

He set to work. Into the tub of hot,

soapy water went one thing after another.
How Pinky rubbed and scrubbed, how
he squeezed and rinsed!

"And now to hang everything out," he
said, putting his wet washing into a
basket. He found his bag of pegs, and
began to peg up all his things, one after
another, on the line. There they flapped
in the wind, as clean as could be!

Pinky went upstairs to lie down and
have a little rest, for he felt rather tired
after his morning's work. He fell fast
asleep – and while he slept the wind got
up.

It began to blow. It blew hard. It blew

harder still. It whistled down the chimney and rattled the windows. It tugged at all Pinky's washing on the line.

"I'll have it off, I'll have it off!" sang the wind and tugged still harder.

It pulled a curtain off the line, blew it into the air, over the wall, and down it fell on a bush in Mr Stamp-About's garden.

Then it tugged at a blanket, and soon that was flying through the air, too. It hung on to a tree, still flapping in the wind. Then off went two cushion-covers – oh dear, what a pity to see them lying on the grass in Mr Stamp-About's garden!

At last the wind whistled so very, very loudly down the chimney that it woke Pinky up. He sat up, wondering what the noise was.

"Oh dear – it's the wind," he said. "I do hope my washing is all right on the line. Why, there's quite a gale blowing!"

He ran to the window – and then he saw that half his lovely clean washing was flapping about in Mr Stamp-About's garden. He groaned.

"I simply must go and get it back," he said. "I can't afford to lose all that."

And then he suddenly saw Mr Stamp-About walking gleefully out into his garden to collect all the wind-blown washing! Pinky flung open the window and called angrily, "You give that back to me! I couldn't help the wind blowing it over the wall."

"If you will throw things into my garden I shall keep them!" shouted back Mr Stamp-About. "Into my kitchen cupboard they'll go!" And he marched indoors with the blanket, the cushion-covers and the curtain. Horrid old Stamp-About!

Pinky went downstairs. He thought of his balls, his aeroplane, his bow and arrows, and his washing. He began to cry. It was too bad. How dare Mr Stamp-About take all his things like that?

Somebody put his head round the door. It was Pop-About, Pinky's cousin, a cheeky little fellow with bright green eyes. "What's up?" he said. "I thought I heard you crying! You're too old to cry. What's the matter?"

Pinky told him. Pop-About sat on the table, swung his legs and listened. "It's a shame," he said. "But why don't you get them back?"

"How can I?" wept Pinky. "I'm very frightened of Mr Stamp-About. He'd stamp on both my feet if I went near him."

"Well – what about getting your things back by a little trick?" said Pop-About, cheerfully. "I'm good at tricks."

"Yes, I know you are," said Pinky. "Well, you just think of a trick this very minute, then!"

Pop-About thought hard. "I know one," he said at last. "Can you lend me a broom?"

"Yes. But what for?" asked Pinky, surprised.

"Well, listen – I'm going to take your broom and go and rap at Stamp-About's door, and tell him I've come to test his kitchen ceiling," said Pop-About, with a grin. "And I'll say I must hold the broom up against the ceiling, while he goes and stamps about on the floor of the room above, to make sure that his kitchen ceiling below is quite safe. You did hear that old Mother Flip-Flap's ceiling fell down yesterday, didn't you?"

"I did," said Pinky. "But I still don't see how this silly-sounding trick is going to get back my things for me."

"Well, while Stamp-About is having a perfectly lovely time stamping about to his heart's content, I'm going to unlock his kitchen cupboard and take out all the things there that belong to you," said Pop-About, with a grin. "And you'll be just outside the window, Pinky, ready to catch them when I throw them!"

"What an idea!" said Pinky, cheering up tremendously. "Come on – let's do it! I'll keep out of sight till you've got Stamp-About upstairs. I say – what a joke!"

Pop-About took a broom, and marched off to Mr Stamp-About's house. He banged at the door. Stamp-About opened it. "Now then, now then," he began.

"Are you Mr Stamp-About?" asked Pop-About. "Did you hear about Mother

Flip-Flap's ceiling falling down yesterday? Well, I'm going round testing people's ceilings for them. There's no charge. Shall I test yours to make sure it's safe?"

"Come in," said Stamp-About, who always liked something for nothing. "How are you going to test it?"

"Well, I am going to stand down here in your kitchen, and hold this very special broom up against the ceiling," said Pop-About. "And I would like you to go upstairs and walk about over the floor of the room above, Mr Stamp-About. Then I shall hold the broom up and see if there is any weakness in your ceiling."

"Right," said Mr Stamp-About. "I'll go. You will hear me all right upstairs!"

"Please stamp round till I call out for you to stop," said Pop-About. In a few moments Stamp-About was upstairs in the room above – and my word, how he stamped around! You might have thought there were a dozen elephants performing up there!

Pop-About let him stamp as much as he liked. He popped over to the cupboard, unlocked it and took out all Pinky's things. He carried them to the window and threw them out to Pinky, who was waiting outside. Balls, arrows, bow, aeroplane, cushion-covers, blanket, curtain, out they all went.

Pinky caught them and scurried home with them, giggling. Pop-About put his broom over his shoulder and followed. He grinned as he heard Stamp-About making more noise than ever upstairs.

"He's enjoying himself all right," he thought. And then, dear me, as Stamp-About did an extra-big stamp, a bit of ceiling came down! It really did. It fell on to the hearth-rug and lay there – and then another piece came down, and another!

Pop-About fled, chuckling. Stamp-About did a little jumping and then got tired. He called down the stairs. "Hey – haven't you tested my ceiling enough?"

There was no answer. Down came Stamp-About in a rage – and, dear me, there was his kitchen cupboard, open and empty – and there was half his ceiling down on the floor!

He rushed to Pinky's at once – but the door was locked. Pinky put his head out of his window. "Go and tell the policeman, if you like," he said, "but all I've done is to take back from you things that belonged to me – and I can't steal what belongs to me! Ha, ha!"

"And by the way," yelled Pop-About, sticking his head out, too, "it's a jolly good thing I tested your ceiling for you, Mr Stamp-About. It was dreadfully dangerous. It fell down. You really must get that mended!"

Well, well – you should have seen Mr Stamp-About stamping down the path in a rage, back to his own cottage! He'll certainly have to mend the holes he stamped in his garden path, as well as the holes in his ceiling – and you may be sure that neither Pinky nor Pop-About will help him!

Clever
Old Budgie

Every evening after tea, Robert and Bessie opened their budgerigar's cage and let out the excited little bird.

"Come on, Budgie, dear little Budgie, spread your wings and fly!" said Robert. "Come on to my head, if you like!"

"Talk, Budgie, talk!" said Bessie. "Say 10345!"

"Don't be silly, Bessie!" said Robert. "What's the sense of teaching our budgie a silly thing like our telephone number!"

"He might escape one day and then if he said our telephone number, somebody might guess what he was saying and telephone us," said Bessie. "It's *not* a silly idea. You're silly to teach him 'Rock-a-bye-baby'. Why don't you teach him a sensible song?"

"Well, he says 'Rock-a-bye' so well," said Robert. "Soon he'll get the whole line – and the tune too! Budgie, listen: 'Rock-a-bye-baby, on the tree-top.'"

"Rock-a-bye, rock-a-bye," said the little green and blue budgie, his head on one side. "10345, rock-a-bye-10345."

"There – you've muddled him with your silly telephone number!" said Robert, crossly. "Please don't teach it to him any more."

"He knows it now," said Bessie. "Ask for your dinner, Budgie! Say, 'Where's my dinner?'"

"Where's my dinner?" said Budgie, in his funny little voice. "Dinner, 10345."

He flew all about the room, sitting on the lampshade, then on the curtain pelmet, then on the top of the clock. Bessie held out her finger and he flew on to it at once, making a funny little noise in his throat.

The budgerigar was very sweet, and very tame. Robert and Bessie loved him, and Robert felt proud whenever the tiny bird flew on to his shoulder and

pretended to whisper in his ear.

Budgie had a lovely cage with a little mirror, and a bell he could ring. Sometimes he rang it so often that Bessie said it sounded as if little Noddy was somewhere in the room, ringing the bell on his blue hat!

One day Joe came to tea, and he couldn't take his eyes off the budgie. *Tinkle-tinkle-tinkle*, went the little bell, and as soon as Joe looked up to the cage the budgie put his pretty head on one side and spoke clearly:

"Rock-a-bye, dinner, dinner, dinner!"

"Isn't he marvellous!" said Joe. "I do wish I had a bird like that! Will he come out of his cage? Is he tame?"

"Oh yes – he always comes out after tea," said Bessie. "He may fly on your head, Joe, so don't be surprised!"

After the tea was cleared away, Mother left the children to amuse themselves. Joe wanted the budgie out of his cage, of course, and Bessie went to get him.

"Shut the window, Joe," she said. "It's open and we musn't let Budgie fly away. He wouldn't know how to feed himself, and he might die."

Joe slid the top part of the window upwards – but he didn't quite shut it. He didn't notice that there was a small space still left at the very top. He was so anxious to see the budgie come out of his cage. Out he came, and flew straight to Robert, sitting on his hand and pecking at his nails. "Dinner, dinner," he said, and Robert laughed.

"No – my nails aren't your dinner. Don't, Budgie!"

Joe spoke to the tiny bird, "Say my name," he said. "Joe, Joe, Joe! Say Joe!"

"10345," said the budgie, his head on one side.

"What's that he said?" asked Joe, surprised.

"It's a silly thing Bessie has taught him to say," said Robert. "Our telephone number! Budgie, say 'Rock-a-bye baby on the tree-top.' Go on, now – you said the whole of it yesterday!"

"No – say Joe, JOE!" said Joe, in such a loud voice that Budgie was frightened. He flew off Robert's hand at once, with a little squeak, and went to the pelmet of the curtain above the window. He stood there, peering down cautiously. Then he felt the little draught that came in through the open space at the top of the window, and flew down to see where it came from.

And in one moment he was gone! He hopped on to the top of the open window, slid through the little space there, spread his wings – and vanished!

Bessie screamed. "Oh! Budgie's gone! Joe, you didn't shut the window properly – you left a crack at the top. Budgie's gone!"

They all raced out into the garden. "Budgie, Budgie, Budgie, where are you? Budgie, come back!" they called.

But no Budgie was to be seen anywhere. Where could he be? The children called him and hunted in the garden from top to bottom till it was dark.

"It's no good," said Robert at last. "He's gone. Goodness knows where! He won't last long because he can't feed himself properly – and a cat might get him. Blow you, Joe – leaving the window a crack open!"

Bessie was in tears. Mother comforted her and went to ring up the police station to report the loss. It was dreadful to think of little Budgie out in the darkness all by himself. He had never been out of doors before. What a big, frightening world it would seem to him.

"Will the other birds help him?" asked

Bessie, tearfully. "Will they show him where to sleep at night? Will they tell him to beware of cats?"

"Perhaps," said Mother. "Now stop worrying about him. Maybe someone will telephone to the police station to say they have found him."

But nobody telephoned the police that night nor the next morning. And then suddenly their own telephone rang, and a voice spoke clearly.

"Hello! Is that 10345?"

"Yes, it is," said Robert, who was answering the telephone because his mother was busy. "Can I take a message to my mother for you?"

"Well – I rang up to know if you had lost a beautiful little budgerigar," said the voice.

"Oh, *yes* – we have!" said Robert. "Is he all right?"

"Well, he's a bit scared," said the voice. "He's in my garden, and he won't let me catch him."

"However did you know he might be ours?" said Robert.

"My little boy saw him first," said the voice, "and when he went out to see what kind of bird was sitting in our plum-tree, the bird spoke to him – he was so surprised – and it said 10345 over and over again. So my little boy came running in and said that the bird must be telling him its telephone number, and please would I telephone to see if a budgie lived at that address!"

"Oh – clever Budgie!" said Robert. "It *is* our telephone number. What's your address? We'll come and fetch him."

"We live at Tall Chimneys, Scotts Lane," said the voice. "I'll tell my little

boy to keep his eye on the budgie till you come. Fancy him knowing his own telephone number!"

Robert ran to tell Bessie and his mother.

"There! I was *very* sensible to make him learn his telephone number, wasn't I?" said Bessie, overjoyed. "Oh quick – let's go and get him. Mummy, will you take us in the car?"

"Of course," said Mother. "Go and open the garage, Robert, while I get my coat. We must go at once, or Budgie might fly away from the garden he's in."

They were soon at Tall Chimneys, where a small boy was waiting for them at the gate. "Hello – you've been quick!" he said, opening the gate to let the car through into the little drive. "Budgie's still here. I almost thought he was going to fly on to my hand once, but he didn't. Come on, he's over here!"

He led the two children down a little path to a summerhouse – and there, sitting on a creeper that climbed all over it, was Budgie!

"Budgie!" called Bessie, excited. "Dear Budgie. We've come to take you home!"

Budgie gave a little squawk of joy and flew straight to Bessie's outstretched hand. She covered him gently with her other hand so that he could not fly away again.

Robert had brought a little travelling-cage with him, and Budgie was soon safely inside and the door shut on him. "10345," he called. "10345."

"There – that's what he kept saying," said the little boy. "At first I didn't know what he was talking about, then suddenly I wondered if he could possibly be saying his telephone number."

"He was! I taught him," said Bessie, red with pride. "But Robert thought it was a silly idea, didn't you, Rob?"

"Yes. But I don't now. I think it was a marvellous idea of yours," said Robert. He turned to the small boy. "Thank you very much for phoning us. We're so glad to get our little budgie safely back!"

And off they went with him, laughing to hear him squawking crossly in his tiny

travelling-cage. How glad he was to see
his own big cage again! He hopped inside,
rang his bell loudly, and looked at himself
in the mirror.

"Rock-a-bye, dinner, dinner," he said.

"It's a good thing you didn't say *that* to
the little boy!" said Bessie. "Clever old
Budgie!"

"Clever old Bessie!" said Mother and
Robert together. And I agree with them
– clever old Bessie!

Do Hurry Up, Mr Twinks!

Mr Twinks was a dreadful sleepy-head. He was always late for everything! He was late for breakfast, lunch, and tea; he was late at the office, he was late going home, and he was late going to bed.

Mrs Twinks got so worried about him. "You know, Twinky," she said to him, "it's such bad manners to be late! Can't you try and be punctual, my dear?"

"What does it matter, being late?" said Mr Twinks, who simply didn't care. "People can wait for me, can't they?"

"Yes – but why should they?" said Mrs Twinks, very worried. "It makes people so cross with you. Now, Twinky dear, do get up when you're called tomorrow and be in time for breakfast. Then you'll be in time for the office too."

Do Hurry Up, Mr Twinks!

But Mr Twinks got up late as usual – dawdled through his breakfast, and dawdled to the office. He was manager of a bookshop, and because he was always late, all the others were late too, even the little office-boy. It was dreadful.

One day the owner of the shop met Mrs Twinks and stopped her in the street.

"Madam," he said, "why don't you get your husband to the shop in good time? Don't you know that he will soon lose his job if he goes on being late? I won't stand it. No – that I won't!"

And Mr Booky dug his walking-stick into the ground and looked so fierce and angry that poor Mrs Twinks felt really frightened. Oh, suppose Mr Twinks did lose his job – whatever would they do?

Mr Booky frowned hard at Mrs Twinks, and went on his way without even saying good-day. Mrs Twinks felt so bad that she went into Dame Goody's cake-shop and sat down for a minute.

"Why, Mrs Twinks, whatever's the matter?" asked Dame Goody.

Mrs Twinks told her all about it. "But there, Dame Goody, what am I to do?" she almost wept. "I can't alter Twinky now, can I? He'll go on being late for things all his life long."

Dame Goody leaned over the counter and whispered into Mrs Twinks's ear, "My dear, go and see Lucy Little at midnight," she said. "She will know what to do for you. She's got a lot of old spells she made when she lived in Pixieland for a while. But don't you tell anyone."

"Oh, thank you," said Mrs Twinks, drying her eyes.

So that night, when Mr Twinks was safe in bed and snoring, Mrs Twinks stole out in the darkness to Lucy Little's cottage at the edge of the wood. Lucy Little opened the door and wasn't at all surprised to see her.

"Come in," she said. "I know what you want – something to stop that lazy husband of yours from being late!"

"Oh, how clever you are, Lucy," said Mrs Twinks, surprised. "Can you help me? I'm so afraid Twinky will lose his job if something isn't done."

"Well, look here, Mrs Twinks, I've a strange little bell that will help Twinky to hurry," said Lucy Little with a sly smile. She picked up something from the table and held out her hand. Mrs Twinks looked at it. She could see nothing.

"Where is it?" she asked.

"Oh, I forgot you couldn't see it," said Lucy. "It's invisible except to people like myself. Now, Mrs Twinks, all you have to do is to take this bell and hang it on to a button or hook or something on Twinky's clothes. Then it will do the rest."

"What will it do?" asked Mrs Twinks.

"You must wait and see," said Lucy Little. "Now, take the bell – you can feel it even if you can't see it."

Mrs Twinks felt about on Lucy's hand and took up a tiny bell. It was funny to pick up something she couldn't see. She thanked Lucy Little and turned to go. "I do so hope it will cure him," she said. "I don't want him to lose his job."

"Lazy fellow!" said Lucy Little. "I only wish I had a bigger bell – but still, this one will be enough to give him a shock!"

Mrs Twinks hurried home. She looked at Twinks's clothes hung over a chair. She decided to hang the bell on one of his trousers' buttons at the back. That would be a good place. So she hung the tiny bell on a button, and then climbed into bed and went to sleep.

Mr Twinks wouldn't get up in the morning, of course! Mrs Twinks called him. She shook him. She even took the bedclothes right off him – but Twinks pulled them up again.

And then a bell began to ring! Goodness, it filled the whole bedroom with its jangling! Twinks shot up in bed and listened. "Must be the fire-bell!" he said. And he was so excited that he dressed himself at once. The bell stopped ringing.

So Twinky slowed down and wasn't nearly ready when the breakfast-bell sounded downstairs. He wasn't going to hurry!

"R-r-r-r-ring! R-r-r-r-r-ring! R-r-r-r-ring!" suddenly went the bell at the back of Mr Twinks. He was wearing it now, on his back trousers' button, though he didn't know it! Twinky jumped in alarm. Why, that bell sounded as if it was in the bedroom!

"R-r-r-r-ring! R-r-r-r-ring!" The bell went on and on, very loudly indeed. Twinks hated it. He hurried downstairs in alarm – and the bell stopped as soon as he hurried.

"My dear, there's a very strange bell or something up in my bedroom," said Twinks, stirring his cocoa.

"Really?" said Mrs Twinks, thinking to herself that it wasn't up in the bedroom now – it was down in the dining-room! "Now hurry, Twinky dear – it would be so nice if you could be early at the office for once."

Twinks didn't hurry, of course. He made a pattern on his porridge with the treacle. He cut his toast into tiny squares and put a dab of marmalade on each. The clock struck nine – he should have been at the office!

"R-r-r-r-r-ring! R-r-r-r-r-ring! R-r-r-ring!" The bell went off like a fire-alarm again, just at Mr Twinks's back. He leaped out of his chair and upset his hot cocoa over his leg.

"Where's that bell?" he yelled. "Where is it? Making me jump like this! Is it the back-door bell? Is it the front-door bell? Make it stop, make it stop!"

"R-r-r-r-r-r-RING! R-r-r-r-r-r-RING!" went the bell even more loudly than ever. Then it altered its sound and went "Jing-jangle-jangle! Jing-jangle-jangle!"

"It's just behind me somewhere!" said Mr Twinks, and he jumped round to see if he could catch it ringing – but of course the bell went with him, on his trousers' button, so no matter how often he turned round, it was always just behind him.

"I shan't finish my breakfast! That bell is taking away my appetite!" shouted Mr Twinks angrily. "I'm off to the shop – and just see if you can't find that tiresome bell and stop it ringing, Mrs Twinks."

Mrs Twinks was giggling. She really couldn't help it. When Twinky had twisted himself about, trying to find the invisible bell, he had reminded her of a cat chasing its own tail, and she chuckled. Ah, Twinky was having to hurry a bit now! There he was, rushing into the hall to get his hat and coat!

The bell stopped ringing as soon as he hurried. Twinks was so glad. It was really dreadful to have a bell ringing so loudly just behind him all the time. He went off without kissing Mrs Twinks goodbye, he was in such a hurry to leave the bell behind in the house; he didn't know he was taking it with him.

He walked quickly for a little way – and then he came to the bus-stop seat. He sat down on it and began to talk to Mr Waitabit, who was sitting there with the morning paper.

At once the bell began to ring again. It

Jing-jangle-jangle!

made Mr Twinks jump so much that he fell off the seat. Mr Waitabit heard it, too, and he gazed round in amazement. "What's that bell?" he said.

"I don't know," said Twinky, in alarm. "I've been hearing it all morning. I thought it was a bell in my house, but it can't be. It's here too!"

"R-r-r-r-ring! R-r-r-r-ring! Jing-jangle-jangle! Jing-jangle-jangle!"

"I can't bear it!" cried poor Mr Twinks, and he tore off to the shop as if a lion was after him!

The bell stopped ringing at once. It was most extraordinary. Twinks fell into a chair and fanned himself. He was beginning to feel quite frightened. "Perhaps I shan't hear it any more now I'm at the shop," he thought. But that bell hadn't finished with him, oh no, it still had quite a lot to do!

Twinks sat on the chair in his little office, fanning himself. He really felt quite tired out with all his hurrying and the bell-ringing. "I'll just have a little rest," he thought.

But the bell didn't think so. No – it set up its loud ringing again at once. "R-r-r-r-ring! R-r-r-r-ring!"

Mr Twinks jumped dreadfully. Where could that bell be? It was somewhere behind him, he was sure! But no matter how quickly he turned round, he could never see a bell anywhere.

"Jing-jangle-jangle!" went the bell. Then it changed its sound again and went "Ding-a-ding-a-ding!"

Every one came rushing into Mr Twinks's office. "Did you ring, sir?" cried the shopman.

"Did you ring, sir?" cried the shopgirl.

"Yes, sir; did you ring, sir?" cried the office-boy.

"No, I didn't," said Mr Twinks crossly. "Go to your work. Some bell must have rung by mistake." He began to tidy his desk and the bell stopped ringing. He sat down to look through his morning letters. They were dull. After a bit he yawned and thought he would go out and get a morning cup of coffee.

But no sooner had he made up his mind to do that, instead of getting on with his work, than the bell began to ring again – goodness, it sounded as loud as the fire-bell!

All the shop assistants came tearing in again at once, gaping in surprise at the loud bell.

"Did you ring, sir?"

"You rang, sir?"

"Yes, sir, yes, sir?"

"Go out, go out!" shouted Mr Twinks in a rage. "No, I didn't ring. I don't know what's ringing. I wish it would stop!"

Everyone went out again, alarmed and

Rrrrr-ring!
Rrrrr-ring!

astonished. Whatever was that bell then, if it wasn't Mr Twinks ringing?

Twinks put on his hat and went out to escape the bell. But it rang loudly behind him all the way to the coffee-shop, and when he got there Mr Twinks felt he really couldn't go into the shop. He began to feel that the bell had something to do with himself. What would people in the shop say if the bell rang all the time?

So Twinks turned back and ran, yes, ran, back to the bookshop! And of course, the bell stopped ringing at once. That seemed rather strange to Mr Twinks. He began to think about it.

"That bell seems to ring when I'm being slow or lazy – and stops when I'm hurrying or working," he thought. "It's funny – very funny."

He went into his office. He picked up his letters and began to answer them. He worked quite hard until it was nearly lunch-time. All his assistants left to go to their lunch and it was time for Twinks to go too. He leaned back in his chair. He was tired. He wouldn't hurry – his lunch could wait!

But – "R-r-r-r-ring! Ding-a-ding-a-ding!" The noise made Mr Twinks leap out of his chair as if he had been shot.

"Be quiet!" he said to the bell. "Be quiet, can't you? I'm going – I'm going as fast as I can!"

"Ding!" said the bell and stopped ringing, for Mr Twinks was now hurrying out of the shop as fast as he could go. He almost ran home – and for the first time in his life was in time for lunch! Mrs Twinks was surprised and pleased.

"That bell has been worrying me a lot this morning," said Twinks. "I've discovered that it rings whenever it thinks I'm being slow – and it stops when I hurry."

"Very peculiar, dear," said Mrs Twinks, handing her husband a plate of hot stew.

"But if that bell thinks it's going to treat me like that, it's mistaken!" said Twinks fiercely. "Ringing at me like that!

Deafening me! Making people turn round and stare – making people rush into my office and shout, 'Did you ring, sir? – Did you ring, sir?' I won't have it!"

"I should think not, Twinky!" said Mrs Twinks, giggling a little to herself, as she thought of all that had happened.

Twinks sat down after lunch to look at the newspaper. He read – and then he shut his eyes and fell asleep. Mrs Twinks didn't wake him. She knew that the magic bell would. And it did!

This time it decided to make a noise like a church bell. So it began.

"Dong! Dong! Dong! Dong!"

Twinks awoke with a start and leaped out of his chair. "Churchtime!" he cried. "We shall be late for church!"

Then he remembered that it was Tuesday and he looked puzzled. "Oh! It's that tiresome bell again! If only I could find it I'd smash it to bits!"

The bell rang loudly like a telephone – "R-ring, r-r-r-ring!" It sounded just as if it were laughing at poor Mr Twinks.

Twinks crammed his hat on his head

and went out to his shop. He was in good time for once, and discovered that not one of his assistants was there. It was two o'clock, and the shop was supposed to be open then – but it was still shut and no one could get in to buy any books, however much they wanted to. Twinks was simply furious.

When at last the three assistants appeared, he was very angry with them. "How long has this lateness being going on?" he cried.

"Just as long as you yourself have been late," said the office-boy cheekily.

"Now, a little more rudeness from you and you'll leave at once!" shouted Mr Twinks, glaring. All the same, it made him think a little. After all, how could he expect his helpers to be early if he was always late himself. It was a shocking example for him to set. Dear, dear! This really wouldn't do!

Twinks worked hard for the rest of the day. He was home in good time for supper. The bell didn't ring once and Mr Twinks was glad. But he spoilt everything by not wanting to go to bed. He sat yawning by the fire, while poor Mrs Twinks tried to make him go upstairs.

"All right, all right, there's no hurry," said Mr Twinks – and then he jumped so much that he trod on the cat's tail and it leaped across the hearth-rug and tripped up poor Mrs Twinks! The bell had begun to ring again!

This time it was like a fire-bell, and what a noise it made. "It'll wake all the neighbours!" cried Mrs Twinks. "Oh dear, oh dear!"

Twinks ran across the room in a hurry. He rushed upstairs and began to undress. The bell stopped ringing at once. Twinky did hope that the fire brigade wouldn't turn out. It was simply dreadful having a bell like that which went off at any time!

Mrs Twinks waited till Twinks was in bed, and then she felt about for the magic bell. She found it, still hanging from one of his trousers' buttons at the back. She took it off. She was sorry for Twinks and thought he had had enough of the bell. Poor Twinky!

Twinks was up early in the morning. He hurried through his breakfast. He

was early at the shop – and who should be there but old Mr Booky, ready to give Mr Twinks a good scolding! But he was so early that Mr Booky was pleased.

"Dear, dear – how punctual you are!" he said to Mr Twinks. "I was going to tell you that you couldn't have your job any longer, because you are always so late – but if you have turned over a new leaf, and are going to be early and hard-working, I will let you keep your job!"

"Oh, Mr Booky, I want to keep my job!" cried Mr Twinks in alarm, glad that he was early for once. "Yes, yes – I have turned over a new leaf – lots of new leaves! I'm always going to be early and quick and hard-working in future, really I am!" And to himself he said, "And I just won't have that tiresome bell ringing at me any more!"

He didn't know the bell was gone. He quite thought it was somewhere about still. And he was so anxious that it shouldn't ring that he hurried and scurried all day long, and really felt very busy and happy.

The bell didn't ring, of course. Mr Twinks had taken it back to Lucy Little – and how Lucy had laughed when she heard what had happened! "I expect he's learned his lesson by now," she said. "It doesn't usually take more than a day, you know. I'm glad you brought the bell back, my dear. A mother has just come in to borrow it. She says she wants it for her child, who is so dawdly and lazy. So I can give it to her, can't I?"

Lucy Little gave the bell to the grateful mother and she hurried off with it – and some child is going to be very, very puzzled by a bell that rings behind him just when he is feeling dawdly. Let me know if it's you, won't you, because I would dearly like to borrow the bell for someone I know!

Billy-
up-the-Tree

"Billy! If I catch you climbing trees again
I'll send you straight to bed!" said his
mother. "Look at your trousers – torn to
bits! And you've got a most enormous
hole in that new jersey. It's very naughty
of you."

"The other boys climb trees," said Billy,
looking sulky.

"The other boys are bigger, they're
more careful, and they only climb when
they have their oldest clothes on," said
his mother. "You may fall – and if you
do you'll break an arm or a leg, and feel
very sorry for yourself indeed. I forbid
you to climb trees until you are older."

Well, that was that. Billy was cross
and upset. But he didn't like to disobey.
His father didn't like boys who disobeyed

their mothers. In fact, he was very stern about it indeed!

Now, a week later, Billy was out in the garden by himself. Tom looked over the wall and grinned.

"Hello! I've been tree-climbing. I got right to the top of a big chestnut. I bet you've never climbed a big tree."

"I have so," said Billy. "We've got a chestnut in our garden. I've climbed that."

"Not to the top," said Tom. "I bet you wouldn't dare."

"I jolly well would," said Billy. "But I've been forbidden to. And anyway, I haven't got my old clothes on."

"You're just making excuses," said Tom and he laughed. "You daren't climb up that tree!"

"All right. You just watch!" said Billy, and he ran to the chestnut tree. Up he went, branch by branch, for the tree was not very difficult to climb. Then – oh dear! – he caught his jumper on a sharp piece and tore it. Bother! Now his mother would be cross again.

"Go on – up to the top," said Tom, sitting on the wall and watching. "That's it. Go right up!"

And soon Billy was at the top of the chestnut tree and could see a very long way indeed. He could see right over the tops of the houses, and as far as the river. The wind blew and the tree swayed a little. Billy felt as if he was on a ship at sea.

"Somebody's coming! I'm going," said Tom, and disappeared. Billy looked down between the branches. He couldn't see anyone – but he could hear somebody whistling. Goodness – it was his father! How dreadful if he was seen.

He sat quite still. After a while Father went indoors again. Then Billy began to climb down the tree. But after going down two or three branches he stopped.

"This isn't the way I came up," he said to himself. "I can't get down this way."

He climbed up again, and then started down a different way. But somehow or other he couldn't get down. No matter how he tried, he couldn't seem to get past one of the branches. His jumper caught again, and another hole was made. Then his trousers caught, and that meant another tear.

Billy began to feel afraid. Suppose he never could get down that tree! He must. He simply must. So he tried again, but it wasn't a bit of good. Either he came to a branch that was right in his way or else he came to such a big drop that he was afraid to try it.

He sat in a fork of the tree and wondered what to do. "I daren't call out for help. If Mum and Dad know I've been climbing again they really will be angry. I wouldn't be surprised if Dad sends me to bed. Oh, how can I get down?"

Well, he couldn't. He just couldn't. And he didn't dare to call for help either. So he sat up there till teatime. He heard his mother calling him, but he didn't dare to answer. He went without his tea. He began to feel very bored and miserable, and very hungry, too.

"Why did I climb this silly tree just to show Tom I could? It's all his fault! How long have I got to stay here?"

It grew cold and Billy shivered. Then, to his horror, it began to grow dark as well. It was evening.

His mother called again. His father came out into the garden to look for him. There he was, almost under the tree, and Billy didn't dare to say a word.

But he couldn't stay there all night, he really couldn't! He began to try to climb down again. Then he got stuck, and couldn't go up or down. The wind got up, and the tree shook.

"It's terribly, terribly cold," said Billy to himself, trying to warm his hands. "Oooh! How the wind blows! The tree is rocking just like a ship. I hope I shan't fall out – though perhaps that's the only way I'll ever get out of this horrible tree!"

By now his mother and father were really worried about Billy. Wherever could he be? Ought they to ring up the police? They couldn't think what to do. Billy never, never missed his tea – and now it was almost supper-time.

Then they heard a miserable voice calling, "Mum! Dad! Help me, help me!"

"That's Billy!" said his mother, clutching his father. "His voice is coming from the garden. Where can he be?"

They ran out and listened. "Where are you, Billy? Where are you?" called his mother.

"Here, Mum, here! Up in the chestnut tree," called Billy, miserably. "And I can't get down. I've been here for hours and hours. What shall I do?"

"Up the tree! And you were forbidden to climb!" said his father's voice. "How far up are you?"

"Almost at the top," said Billy. "And I'm so cold."

"I'll get a ladder," said his father. Billy was so glad to hear that. Of course – a ladder! He hadn't thought of that. He had been worrying and worrying how he was ever to get down.

Father fetched the ladder. He put it up against the tree, running it between the broad, spreading branches. The tip of it reached Billy's feet.

He began to climb down. "Now, be careful!" called his father. "It's dark. Go slowly."

Billy's hands were so cold and his feet so icy that he could hardly feel the rungs of the ladder. And quite suddenly he slipped and fell. His father tried to catch him, but couldn't. Then a dreadful pain

ran through Billy's leg and he yelled out, "I'm hurt! My leg, oh, my leg!"

Yes, his poor leg was broken. He had to go to hospital to have it set, and Billy was so frightened and upset that he couldn't help crying.

"No football for you for some time, old son," said the doctor. "No games at all!" He went, and Billy's parents came to sit beside him. Billy told them all about it – how he had climbed because of what Tom said – and then had been too afraid to call for help – and had got so very, very cold.

"Now you'll punish me, and that will make me feel worse than ever," said Billy.

"We don't need to punish people who have punished themselves much harder than we would ever have punished them," said his father. "No football – no games of any sort – that is a dreadful punishment for someone who is so good at them. We are as sad as you are, Billy.

We had so much looked forward to seeing you play in football matches."

"I've spoilt everything," said Billy. "I'm sorry. And how Tom will laugh!"

But Tom didn't. He was upset, too, and he came every day to sit with Billy, and he helped him to walk, too, when he was given crutches.

Now Billy's leg is all right again, and he is running about as fast as ever. And today his mother told him he could climb trees – he really was quite big enough.

"But never climb one you can't get down!" she said. "And if you do, then yell for help!"

But somehow poor Billy doesn't want to climb trees any more. What a shame!

The Enchanter's Poker

"Look what I've got!" said Scally to Wag. Wag looked.

"Ooooh – it's the enchanter's magic poker, isn't it? You'll get into trouble when he misses that, Scally!"

"He's away. His house is empty," said Scally. "So I slipped in to borrow it, just till he comes back, Wag. I can return it when he's home. But think how useful it will be to us!"

"How?" asked Wag.

"Well, who has to go and cut wood for the fire each day? We do. Who has to bring in the logs? We do. Who has to put them on the fire and keep making it up? We do. Well – the poker will see to the fire now!" Scally grinned all over his face.

"Oh, I see. We make up the fire with

wood – and then, whenever it burns down, we stick the poker into it, say a magic word, and it makes the fire burn again, without any fresh wood!" said Wag. "Yes – a very good idea – no more wood cutting for us – just the magic poker at work. Good!"

The two imps lived with their old Aunt Mutter. She was cross and strict and didn't stand any nonsense at all. She worked them very hard – but now they could skip off to play instead of cutting wood. Hurrah!

"Put it by the fireplace," said Wag. "It's so like Aunt Mutter's poker that she'll never notice the difference."

Scally stood the magic poker by the

fireplace and hid the other poker in a cupboard. "The fire's going down," said Wag. "Let's see how this poker does its work. What's the magic word, Scally?"

Scally whispered it to him. The poker heard it and stirred. It hopped to the fire, gave it a violent poke, and hopped back again to its place. The fire blazed up and crackled merrily!

"Goodness – it's better than I thought!" said Scally. "We just say the word – and the poker does the trick. Wonderful!"

"Shh! Here's Aunt Mutter," said Wag, as his plump, sharp-eyed aunt came in. She looked at the fire.

"Ah – burning up well – and a good thing for you it is! There's more wood needed, so go and cut it. I'm going to take a snooze in my chair."

The two imps ran out, chuckling. Cut wood? Not they! Aunt Mutter sat herself down and took up her knitting. The fire died down a little, and the poker knew it ought to poke it. It stirred a little and Aunt Mutter looked up.

"What's that noise? Just the fire, I suppose. Dear me, I'm sleepy. I think I'll take a nap."

She put down her knitting and shut her eyes. She snored a little.

Soon the fire died down a little more, and the poker got quite uneasy. It knew it ought to poke the fire. But it couldn't unless somebody said the magic word. Where were those imps who knew the word?

The poker suddenly left its place by the fire and hopped on its one leg round the kitchen. Hop-hop-hoppitty-hop! It

made quite a noise on the stone floor. Aunt Mutter woke up with a jump.

"Now who's that? Is it you, Scally and Wag, hopping about? Just keep still or I'll give you something to make you hop still more!"

The poker hid behind the dresser, waiting till Aunt Mutter fell asleep again. Then out it came and hopped to the window. It looked out. Where were Scally and Wag?

They didn't come and the fire almost went out. The poker got very worried indeed. Perhaps Aunt Mutter knew the magic word? It hopped cautiously over to her and poked her in the leg.

She woke up at once and rubbed her leg. "What was that? Was it you, Puss, rubbing against me? Leave me alone, do!"

She shut her eyes again, and slept. The poker gave her a jab on the other leg and Aunt Mutter sat up with a yell.

"What's happening? Stop it! Jabbing me like this!" She looked all round but she couldn't see the poker, which was hiding under an armchair. The cat wasn't there either. Aunt Mutter began to feel very puzzled.

Bang-bang! That was somebody knocking at the door. "Come in!" called Aunt Mutter.

In came old Mr Shuffle, beaming all over his face. "Just come to say how-do-you-do," he said.

"Ah, that's nice of you. Sit down in the armchair there," said Aunt Mutter. "I'll put the kettle on for a cup of tea. Dear, dear – the fire's gone down low. Where's the poker?"

The poker wasn't there, of course. It was under the armchair, and Mr Shuffle was at that very moment sitting down in the chair, making it creak loudly.

Aunt Mutter was cross. No poker – no wood to put on the fire – and no Scally and Wag to bring some in, either. Dear, dear – she'd never get the kettle to boil on a fire like that.

She opened a cupboard door – and there was her poker – the one that Scally and Wag had hidden when they had brought in the magic one. Aunt Mutter was surprised to see it there. She took it and poked up the fire briskly. Then she put some coal on as there was no wood.

The poker under the chair tried to get out when it saw Aunt Mutter using another poker. Mr Shuffle heard it and looked down. "I think your cat must be under here," he said. "I can feel her struggling to get out."

"Now don't you get up," said Aunt Mutter. "Puss can easily get out if she wants to. She shouldn't get under chairs. I think she must have been under mine

this afternoon – jabbing her claws into my leg!"

The poker grew desperate. It gave Mr Shuffle a hard poke, and Mr Shuffle almost jumped out of his skin.

"Your cat's trying to bite me or something," he said. "Oooh – there it goes again – why, it's jabbing me. Has it gone mad, do you think?"

"Bless us all, I hope not!" said Aunt Mutter, alarmed. "Get up, Mr Shuffle, before she does you any damage. Move your chair."

So Mr Shuffle got up and moved his chair. The magic poker hopped out at once and went to Aunt Mutter, who

135

stared in alarm. "What's this? A poker – a hopping poker? Get away, you tiresome thing!"

The poker hopped all round her, longing for her to say the magic word that would make it poke the fire so that it would burn brightly. She was frightened and poured water over it from the kettle. Then it hopped to Mr Shuffle, and he went and hid himself in a cupboard. He simply couldn't bear pokers that acted like that.

Then in came Scally and Wag, thinking that it must be teatime. The poker jigged over to them, and they stared in horror. Why – Aunt Mutter's own poker now stood by the fireplace, and the magic one was hopping about for everyone to see. What would Aunt Mutter say if they told her they had taken it from the enchanter's empty house? She would be very, very angry.

"Scally! Wag! Where did this poker come from?" cried their aunt. "It's gone completely mad."

"I don't know anything about it," said

Scally, most untruthfully. "It must have escaped from some witch or some wizard, Aunt. I'll chase it out-of-doors."

But it was the poker who chased Scally, and jabbed at him so hard that he yelled. In the end Wag took a stick and hit the poker. It fell over, and Scally kicked it out of the kitchen. He slammed the door. Wag looked out of the window.

"It's hopping away," he said. He whispered in Scally's ear. "It's gone back to the enchanter's house, I expect."

There was no further sign of the poker, and everyone sat down to tea. Scally and

Wag were rather scared afterwards when their aunt sent them out to get in more wood. Suppose that poker was lying in wait for them?

But it wasn't. They brought in some wood, and hoped that Aunt Mutter wouldn't notice that there was now very little in the woodshed. Mr Shuffle said good evening and went. The two imps wondered whether the poker would see him and chase him. But no doubt it was standing safely in its own fireplace by now.

Now, when they were in bed that night, Wag woke up with a jump. He sat up and listened. *Tap-tap-tappitty-tap! Tap-tap-tappitty-tap!* He could hear a tapping noise quite distinctly in the yard outside. Oh, dear – could it be the poker back again? Wag woke Scally and the two lay and listened to the tappitty noise outside.

Their bedroom was on the ground floor, and very soon there came a tapping noise at the window. *Tap-tap-tappy-tappy-tap!*

"It's that poker back again!" whispered

Wag. "It will break the window! We'd better let it in and stand it by the fireplace. Bother it!"

So Wag opened the window, and in hopped the poker. It was shivering. It had been all the way back to the enchanter's house but it couldn't find any place to get in. So it had come back to stand by Aunt Mutter's warm fire.

But there was no fire. It had gone right out. The poker had a look at it and hopped all the way back from the kitchen to the imps' bedroom.

"It's back again," said Scally, in despair. It hopped up on to the bed, slithered between the warm blankets and lay there, stiff and straight.

"We can't have it in bed with us!" said Wag, and kicked it out. But it was back again in a second and gave him such a jab that he cried out in pain.

It was a dreadful night for the imps. Every time they moved the poker jabbed them – and in the early morning it pushed and poked them till they had to get out of bed and dress. It wanted them to make the fire and light it, so that it could go and stand in the warmth, where it usually stood. Poor Scally and Wag, they had never been up so early in their lives before!

Aunt Mutter saw the poker standing quietly beside her own poker at the side of the fireplace. She gaped in surprise. "You don't mean to say it's back again!" she said. "Wag and Scally, just tell me truthfully – where did that poker come from?"

Scally began to cry, because he was

black and blue where the poker had
jabbed him in the night. He told his aunt
all about the magic poker, and she was
full of horror.

"What! It belongs to the enchanter –
and you've been using its magic? What do
you suppose he will say when he hears?
Why, he might quite well change you
both into pokers yourselves, and then
what would you do?"

The poker thought this was very funny
and shook with laughter, though it didn't
make a sound. Scally and Wag glared at
it. Horrid thing – sleeping with them,

and jabbing them – and now laughing. They couldn't even use it now, for they didn't dare to say the magic word.

"Oh, Aunt Mutter – what shall we do? The enchanter is away, so we can't give him back the poker," wept Wag. "And we can't put up with it here."

"Oh, yes, we can," said Aunt Mutter. "Hey, poker! You can stay here till your master comes back, and we won't use your magic at all – but let me tell you this – if you want to chase these two bad imps and make them do their work well, I'd be glad. You do that!"

The poker shook with laughter again, and hopped out from the fireplace at once. It chased Scally to the sink to make him begin the washing-up, and it chased Wag outside to fetch some wood. Aha! It was going to have a very fine time.

Aunt Mutter is very pleased with it. In fact, she is thinking of buying it from the enchanter when he returns. That would be a shock for Scally and Wag!

Simple Simon
Makes a Mistake

"Listen to me, Simon," said his mother one day. "I am going to take Baby to see Auntie Harriet. I shall leave you at home to look after Rover and Sally-cat. So you must be a good boy and not get into mischief."

"No, Mummy," said Simon. "I won't get into mischief. I promise I'll be good."

"And just see that Rover and Sally-cat behave themselves too," said Mother. "I don't want to find Rover's muddy paw-marks all over my clean kitchen floor. And please don't let Sally-cat get into the larder."

"Oh no, Mummy," said Simon.

"Well, goodbye, Simon," said Mother, pushing the pram down the path with Baby inside. "Just remember what I've said. You know what happens to naughty boys, don't you? They get sent to bed!"

"Oh yes, Mummy," said Simon, and he waved to his mother till she was out of sight.

Simon felt good that day. He wanted to be helpful and kind and nice. He pulled a mat straight in the kitchen. He went to the larder and looked to see if the lid of the bread bin was on. He opened the oven door to see if the dinner his mother had left cooking was quite all right. Yes, really, Simon was feeling very good.

Rover the dog barked in the yard – Woof, woof, woof! Simon went to the kitchen door and looked out at him.

"You'd better be good, Rover," he called. "You know what happens when we are naughty, don't you? We get sent to bed!"

"Woof, woof!" said Rover, and he ran out into the muddy lane. Something rubbed against Simon's legs. He looked down. It was Sally the cat. Simon bent down and stroked her.

"You'd better be good too, Sally-cat,"

said Simon. "You know what happens when we are naughty, don't you? We get sent to bed!"

"Miaow!" said Sally-cat, and she ran back to the kitchen fire. Simon went down the garden to see if there were any snowdrops peeping out. But he couldn't find any. It was cold so he went back to the kitchen.

And what do you think? Rover was in the kitchen, and had left two trails of muddy paw-marks all across his mother's clean floor. Oh dear! Simon stared at Rover in anger.

"Rover! Didn't I tell you to be good? Didn't I tell you what happens when we

are naughty? You must go straight to bed! Come here!"

Rover wouldn't come. So Simon ran to him and took him by the collar. He dragged the surprised dog up the stairs and into his own bedroom. He turned back the sheet and the blankets and lifted up the heavy dog. *Plonk!* Simon dropped him in the bed and tucked him in tightly.

"Now you just stay there for the rest of the day!" said Simon. "You will not muddy the kitchen again, I am sure!"

He marched downstairs, feeling very important to think he had sent naughty dog Rover to bed. And when Simon got into the kitchen, what did he see but Sally the cat in the larder eating up the meat-pie that Mother had made for his father's supper! My goodness me!

"Sally-cat! How dare you!" he shouted, quite forgetting it was he who had left the larder door open. "Didn't I tell you to be good? Didn't I tell you what happens when we are naughty? You must go straight to bed! Come here!"

146

Sally-cat tried to jump out of the window, but Simon caught her. He did not smack her, and Sally thought he was cuddling her, so she began to purr.

"No, I am not pleased with you, Sally-cat," said Simon. "I am going to send you to bed!"

Up the stairs he climbed, and went into his bedroom. Rover was still in bed, but you should have seen the muddy marks he had made on the clean sheet! And will you believe it, he had chewed a hole in the blanket! But Simon was so cross with Sally-cat that he didn't notice what Rover had done. He pushed the cat down under the clothes and pulled the blanket up tightly. Then he left the dog and the cat together in bed and shut the door. *Bang!* Down the stairs he went and cleared up the bits of meat-pie and washed up the muddy marks on the kitchen floor. He was really feeling a very good boy indeed that day!

But upstairs, oh dear! Sally-cat didn't like being pushed down under the bedclothes with Rover the dog. They were quite good friends usually, but it was strange to be in Simon's bed. Sally-cat scratched Rover's hind leg.

"Woof!" said Rover in alarm. He dived down under the clothes and tried to bite Sally-cat. Sally-cat scratched his nose. Then what a muddle there was in Simon's bed! The dog and the cat got all tangled up in the bedclothes and couldn't get out! They scrambled round this way and they got tied up that way, and they scratched and bit at the blankets and sheets in fright.

But the door was shut, and Simon heard nothing. He got a book and sat down to read quietly. He was quite surprised when the door opened and his mother came home again with Baby.

"Oh, Mummy, I've been such a good boy," said Simon. "I haven't got into any mischief at all."

"That's fine," said his mother, putting Baby into her high chair.

"But Mummy, Rover was very naughty," said Simon. "He walked all across the kitchen floor with his muddy feet."

"And who left the kitchen door open so that he could do that?" said Mother at once.

Simon pretended not to hear. "And Mummy, Sally-cat was naughty too," he said. "She got into the larder and ate the meat-pie there!"

"And who left the larder door open so that she could do that?" said Mother, very cross indeed.

"Well, Mummy, you'll be glad to know that I punished them both," said Simon. "I sent them to bed!"

"To bed!" said his mother. "Whatever do you mean, Simon?"

"I put them both to bed for the rest of the day," said Simon proudly. "They are upstairs in my bed, Mummy, and I'm sure they are feeling very sorry they've been so naughty."

"Oh dear, oh dear, oh dear," said Mother, and she rushed upstairs and into Simon's bedroom! What a sight she saw! There seemed to be a sort of earthquake going on in Simon's bed, and woofs and mews came from it in a most remarkable manner! Rover and Sally-cat were in a dreadful muddle there and were trying their very hardest to get out.

"The sheets are all covered in mud and are torn to bits!" cried Mother. "And the blankets are nibbled and torn! Oh dear, oh dear, oh dear! Shoo, Rover! Shoo, Sally-cat!"

Mother pulled the sheets and blankets off, and the dog and the cat fled downstairs in a hurry. Mother called Simon. He ran upstairs and looked at his torn and dirty bed in surprise.

"Simon, I'm going to send *you* to bed!" said Mother in her crossest voice. "Hurry up and get in! It's all dirty and torn, but that's your own fault. Putting the cat and the dog to bed indeed! Whatever will you think of next! Into bed you get, and there you'll stay all day long!"

"But, Mummy, I was feeling such a good boy!" wailed poor Simon.

"You've got to *be* good as well as feel good!" said Mother.

And so poor Simon stayed in bed, and not even Rover or Sally-cat came to see him! But I'm not surprised at that, are you?

Mr Smick
Plays a Trick

"Now, listen, Smick," said Mrs Smick, "you're to be home in time for your lunch today. Monday you were late and the stew was spoiled. Tuesday you didn't come in till half past two, and the joint was ..."

"Yes, dear, yes, dear," said Mr Smick hastily. "You've told me all that before. I'll be in time today."

"You won't," said Mrs Smick, with a sigh. "You simply haven't any idea of time at all, Smick. And I gave you such a nice watch for Christmas, too."

"Well, don't I always wear it?" said Mr Smick.

"Yes, always. But you hardly ever wind it up, do you?" said Mrs Smick. "So it never tells you the right time! Anyway, if it did you'd forget to look at it."

"I'll be in time today," promised Mr Smick.

"You know your Aunt Melia is coming," said Mrs Smick, "and your sister Mandy. I can't keep lunch waiting for you. I know what you are like when you get to the market – you just wander round and poke your stick at the pigs, and rub the noses of the horses, and pull the wool of the sheep – and you never once think that lunch will be ready at one o'clock sharp."

"I'd better be going," said Mr Smick, who knew that his wife would go on like this for hours if he didn't go.

He took his stick and found his hat. Then just as he was going out, Mrs Smick called him. She had a sly smile on her face.

"Smick! Here, put the bedroom clock into your pocket. It's an alarm clock, and I've set it for half past twelve. It'll go off with a ring then, and you will know it's time to set off home. You'll be in time for lunch for once!"

"Oh dear!" said Smick, who really

didn't want to carry alarm clocks about with him. "All right. I'll put it in my pocket, and I daresay it will remind me to set off back home when it rings."

He put it into his pocket and walked down the garden path to the front gate. He found his small boy swinging on the gate.

"Hello, Dad!" said Jiminy. "Going to the market? I wish you'd bring me back a present. You forgot last time."

"So I did," said Mr Smick. "Well, I really will remember this time. What do you want?"

"A toy telephone," said Jiminy. "Dad, could you get one? I do want one."

"But you can't really telephone with a toy telephone," said Mr Smick. "It's a bit silly. You can only talk into it, and never get a reply from anyone."

"I can pretend I'm talking to somebody who is talking back to me," said Jiminy. "That's all I need to do. Go on, Dad – buy me one if you can."

"Right," said Mr Smick. "I will." Off he went, over the fields, up the hill, and through the wood to the market in the next town.

On the way he met Mr Smack. "Hello, Smick," said Smack. "Just a word of warning. Those three robbers are about again – you know, the three who set on old Mr Sniff the other day and robbed him of his money. It's my belief they've got their hide-out somewhere in the wood."

"Dear me," said Mr Smick, alarmed. "I'll be careful then. I've got to go through the wood. I wish Mr Plod the policeman would get hold of them."

Nasty little creatures they are."

He went on, keeping a sharp look-out as he walked through the wood. But he saw and heard nobody. He got to the market and smiled with pleasure to sniff the good smell of animals, and hear the bleatings and mooings and neighings. Ah, this was good! Plenty going on in the market!

He had a very happy time there, and then he suddenly remembered the toy telephone he had promised to take home to little Jiminy. He'd better get it at once.

He found a toyshop – and what a lucky thing, it had a toy telephone to sell. It was just the thing, with a place to speak into, and a place to listen to with your

ear. It had a little stand with a dial, and
a long piece of black wire. Splendid!
Jiminy would love that.

"I'll buy this," said Mr Smick, and put
his hand in his pocket to get his money.
He touched something round and hard.
Whatever could it be?

Then he remembered. Of course – it
was the bedroom clock that Mrs Smick
had given him to put into his pocket. She
had set the alarm to go off at half past
twelve.

Mr Smick looked hastily at the clock in
the toyshop. He sighed with relief. It was
only ten past twelve. That tiresome clock
wouldn't start ringing yet.

He made up his mind to set off home
before it did. His friends in the market
would laugh at him if they heard the
alarm clock ringing in his pocket. So after
he had paid for the telephone and tucked
it under his arm, he walked through the
market, and set off on his way home.

He came to the wood. He remembered
what Mr Smack had told him about the
robbers. Oh dear! The sun had gone in,

the sky was black with clouds and it seemed very dark indeed under the trees.

"Robbers might be waiting for me anywhere," thought Mr Smick, feeling rather nervous.

Then he heard the blackbird singing loudly nearby.

"Smick, Smick, Smick! Mind how you go, mind how you go! R-r-r-r-r-robbers are near, near, near. R-r-r-r-robbers! Smick, Smick, Smick!"

Smick was most alarmed. Robbers! They would set on him and rob him. He had a lot of money in his pockets, too.

He heard whispering nearby. He felt sure he could see the top of a stick, and the point of somebody's hat behind a bush. He stopped in fright.

"Anyway, they shan't get Jiminy's little telephone," he thought, and he put it up into the tree nearby. And just at that very moment out leaped the three nasty little robbers with yells and shouts. They were goblins, and they had sticks that they flourished in a very horrid way.

"Give us your money!" they cried, and they ran at Mr Smick.

It was exactly half past twelve. The alarm clock in Mr Smick's pocket went off at once, and the alarm rang loudly.

"R-r-r-ring! R-r-r-ring! R-r-r-ring!"

The three robbers stopped in astonishment. They had no idea that Mr Smick had an alarm clock in his pocket, of course.

"A telephone ringing!" said one robber.

"Here in the woods!" cried another.

"What an extraordinary thing!" said the third.

And indeed, the alarm clock did sound exactly like a telephone ringing:

"R-r-r-r-r-r-ring! R-r-r-r-r-ring!"

Then Mr Smick had a most marvellous idea, the best he had ever had in his life.

"Pardon me," he said politely to the surprised robbers. "That's the telephone ringing. Permit me to answer it before you rob me."

"Yes. Yes, certainly," said the biggest goblin, anxious to see where this mysterious telephone was.

Mr Smick reached up to the tree where he had put the toy telephone. He took down the receiver and put it to his mouth and ear.

"Hello!" he said, just as if he were Jiminy having a pretend talk to somebody. "Hello! I can't quite hear you. Who is it?"

He paused as if he were listening to someone at the other end. The three robbers gaped at him. A telephone up a tree in the middle of the woods! Whoever had heard of such a thing? How truly remarkable!

"Oh, Mr Plod – it's you – Mr Plod, the policeman," said Mr Smick. "Good morning, Mr Plod. Smick here, Mr Tobias Smick. What can I do for you?"

The three robbers backed away a little. Good gracious! Could that really be their enemy, Mr Plod the policeman, on the telephone?

"Yes, Mr Plod. Three robbers, did you say? Yes. They've just set on me – nasty little creatures they are. You want them caught, do you? Well, I'll tell you exactly where I am in the wood, and you can send three men here to get them. Or

better still, surround the wood. What, you are coming along yourself too, Mr Plod? Oh, fine, fine!"

The robbers turned pale. They looked at one another. Mr Plod was coming. He was sending men to catch them. The wood might be surrounded!

"Yes, Mr Plod," said Mr Smick. "I'll stay here with them till you come. They want to rob me so that will take a little time – and by then you should have been able to surround the wood. You've no idea what nasty, ugly little things they are."

Mr Smick was enjoying himself tremendously. He had no idea that it was such fun to pretend like this. No wonder Jiminy liked it! He glanced round to see whether the robbers were trembling and shivering.

There was nobody there! One by one the bad little creatures had slipped away between the bushes, afraid of seeing Mr Plod arriving at any minute. Mr Smick was alone.

He gave a sigh of relief. He popped the toy telephone under his coat and set off home, grinning whenever he thought of his pretend telephone call. Dear, dear, how he had enjoyed that!

He got home punctually at one, and

Mrs Smick was very pleased with him. "Good!" she said. "The alarm clock was a very good idea, Smick. Your aunt and your sister are out in the garden waiting for you. Tell them lunch is ready."

"The alarm clock was a much better idea than you knew, my dear," said Mr Smick. "Where's Jiminy? I've got a toy telephone for him – and a wonderful story to tell, as well!"

The three goblins never robbed anyone again. They were so afraid of telephones ringing in the wood! They went back to the tree in which Smick had put the toy telephone – but they never found it, of course.

And that wasn't surprising because it's in Jiminy's playroom, and you'd be surprised at the telephone calls he makes every day. He rings up all kinds of people and talks away to them – he spoke to the King the other day, and to the Lord Chancellor. He'll probably ring me up too, if he thinks of it.

He'd get a surprise if you answered, wouldn't he?

She Forgot to Say Thank You!

There was once a spoilt little girl who always forgot to say thank you when she went out to tea.

We all know that when we say goodbye at the end of a tea party we must say "Thank you for having me and for giving me such a lovely time," and Lucy knew it, too. But she never remembered to say it to people.

"What a pity that Lucy doesn't have good manners," Mrs Brown said. "Do you know, I asked her to tea yesterday with Ken and Anne and when she went she never so much as said thank you!"

"And when I took her for a picnic with Tom and Ellen, and paid for her to have a ride on a donkey on the sands, she went home without a word of thanks!"

said Mrs Jones. "Funny, isn't it? Surely all children know they must say thank you when they have been to somebody's tea party or picnic?"

Aha, but wait! There came a time when Lucy forgot once too often. It happened like this.

She was walking through the wood on her way home from her granny's when a small man ran round a tree and bumped hard into her.

"Oooh," said Lucy. "Do look where you're going. You've broken the egg in this bag. I was taking it home for my breakfast tomorrow. My granny's hen laid it for me."

"Dear me! I'm most terribly sorry," said the brownie. "Er – I don't know if you've realised it, but I'm a brownie – one of the Little Folk, you know. I must certainly make up to you for breaking your precious egg."

"How?" asked Lucy, beginning to feel excited.

"Well, would you like to come to a party this afternoon?" said the brownie. "I'm giving one for six of my friends. It's my birthday, and I'm having a lovely birthday cake with two hundred and thirty-three candles on it."

"Gracious! Are you as old as that?" said Lucy, astonished.

"That's not very old for a brownie," said the little man. "My grandfather is much, much older than that – five hundred and something – I forget exactly. Well, will you come to my party? Three o'clock, and meet me by the big oak-tree over there."

"Oh, yes," said Lucy, and she ran happily home. She had her lunch by herself because her mother was out. She

168

put on a clean dress at half past two and
did her hair nicely. Then she set out for
the big oak-tree.

The brownie was there. He took her
through the wood to a little clearing.
There was a small village there with
quaint little crooked houses, and the
tiniest cats and dogs Lucy had ever seen.

The brownie took her into one of the
houses. There were six of his friends
there and they all shook hands most
politely with Lucy.

On the table was a magnificent
birthday cake. You should have seen it!

Lucy had never in her life seen such a beauty. "Well!" she said. "What a lot of candles! Are there really two hundred and thirty-three? I'd never be able to count them all."

They looked lovely when they were lit. The brownie didn't light them with matches but with his wand. He waved it over the cake and every candle lit at once!

The tea was quite delicious. There were sixteen different kinds of sandwiches, five different kinds of buns, seven kinds of biscuits and the birthday cake. After that there were rainbow jellies, shimmering with seven colours, and ice creams that were colder than any Lucy had ever tasted before.

After tea they played all kinds of lovely games. Then there was a bran-tub to dip into, and every guest got a present. Lucy had a tiny musical box. She loved it.

Then it was time to go. One by one the guests shook hands with the generous little brownie. "Thank you for having us and for giving us such a wonderful time," they said, very politely. "It's been lovely!"

Then it was Lucy's turn to say goodbye. She shook hands, and ran down the path. As usual she forgot to say thank you for the lovely time.

But the path led right back to the brownies' village! There she was again, outside the brownie's house. He came hopefully to the door, expecting that the little girl had remembered her manners and had come to thank him. But she hadn't!

"Bother!" she said. "I must have taken the wrong path."

And off she went again – but in twenty minutes time she was back in the village once more. How very extraordinary!

The brownie came to the door at once, quite expecting Lucy to say she was sorry for having forgotten to thank him for his lovely party. But she didn't. She just stamped her foot crossly and went off again.

But no matter what path she took she always came back to the brownies' village. Soon she began to feel frightened. She called to the brownie.

"What's happening? I can't seem to go home. Every path leads me back here. Why is it?"

"Well – I think it means you've forgotten something," said the brownie. "You see, the paths leading from our village are strange. They always bring people back here if they've forgotten

something. They brought my grandfather straight back when he forgot his umbrella."

"But I haven't forgotten anything at all," said Lucy, crossly. "I didn't have a hat – or a bag – or an umbrella."

"Strange," said the brownie. "It's true, you didn't. You haven't left anything behind at all. What can you have forgotten?"

"I simply don't know," said Lucy. "Think hard, brownie. What have I forgotten?"

The brownie thought hard. Then he went rather red. "Well," he said, "I hardly like to tell you. It's only a little

173

thing, and it's very odd that the paths keep bringing you back for that. But it's the only thing I can think of."

"Well, tell me," said Lucy. "Why don't you like to tell me? It's not anything dreadful."

"It is something rather dreadful," said the brownie. "I feel ashamed to tell you because it will make you feel ashamed, too."

"Oh, do tell me!" cried Lucy, getting impatient.

"It's your manners you have forgotten," said the brownie. "You forgot to say thank you to me for my party. Everyone else remembered, of course, because they've all been well brought up – but you forgot. Still, perhaps you haven't been well brought up, poor child."

Now it was Lucy's turn to go bright red. "I have been well brought up," she said in a small voice. "I do know I ought to say thank you. I'm very, very sorry I forgot. It was dreadful of me after such a lovely party. Thank you, brownie, for having me, and for giving me such a wonderful time."

"That's all right," said the brownie, looking pleased. "I was rather afraid you hadn't enjoyed yourself when you didn't say thank you. I'm glad you did."

"Goodbye, and I do hope I shall see you again," said Lucy, trying to be as nice as ever she could to make up for forgetting her manners. "I'll bring you a bit of my own birthday cake when I have it next week."

She ran off down the path – and will you believe it, it took her safely all the way home! So it was quite clear that it was her manners she had forgotten, and that was why the paths kept taking her back to the village.

The week after that Lucy had a birthday party of her own – and the next day she took a piece of her cake to give to the kind little brownie. But wasn't it a pity, she simply couldn't remember the way to his village.

Still, there was one thing she always did remember after that – and you know what it was, don't you? Yes – she *always* remembered to say thank you after a party!

The Very
Safe Place

Mr and Mrs Tick-Tock lived in a nice little house called Celandine Cottage. Its walls were as gold as the spring celandines, and all the pots and pans inside were as brightly polished as the faces of those lovely little flowers.

Mr and Mrs Tick-Tock were very happy. They only ever quarrelled when they lost anything – and dear me, they always seemed to be losing things!

If Mr Tick-Tock wanted the key of the garden shed in a hurry, and couldn't find it, Mrs Tick-Tock wouldn't know where it was at all! It might be on the mantelpiece – it might be in her bag – or it might be in the kitchen drawer! She would have to hunt and hunt and hunt and by the time she had found it perhaps

177

Mr Tick-Tock had gone out for a walk!

Then very often Mrs Tick-Tock would want some potatoes dug up out of the garden, and she wouldn't be able to find the spade. How she hunted! Then she would ask Mr Tick-Tock where it was, and he would go and look in the shed, or perhaps in the scullery, or maybe out in the field. There was no knowing where it would be.

Mr Tick-Tock would get very angry with Mrs Tick-Tock and Mrs Tick-Tock would get very angry too. They were such a nice couple that it was a pity to see them so cross.

One day Mr Tick-Tock came home with a very large smile on his face.

"What's the matter?" asked Mrs Tick-Tock. "You look very happy."

"Then I look what I am," said Mr Tick-Tock. "See what I've had given to me!"

He held out two bright red tickets and Mrs Tick-Tock gave a scream of delight.

"Ooooh! Tickets for the circus! Oooh! How lovely!"

"They are for Saturday night," said

Mr Tick-Tock. "Won't it be fun?"

"We musn't lose them, whatever we do," said Mrs Tick-Tock anxiously. "You musn't carry them about in your pocket, Tick-Tock. If you do you might pull them out with your handkerchief, and that would be dreadful, for they would flutter to the ground and be lost."

"Well, we must put them in a safe place then," said Mr Tick-Tock. "Where shall we put them?"

Mrs Tick-Tock looked all round the kitchen, frowning hard.

"What about inside the lemonade jug?" she said. "It's made of glass and we could see the tickets quite well through the glass."

"No, that's a silly place," said Mr Tick-Tock. "We might want to use the lemonade jug, then we'd have to take the tickets out."

So they thought again. Mr Tick-Tock suddenly smiled and pointed to the biscuit tin.

"Let's put the tickets there," he said. "It's quite empty, and we never eat biscuits, so they will be safe there. Then when Saturday comes we shall know they are waiting for us in the biscuit tin and we shan't have to hunt all over the place for them!" So they put the red circus tickets in the old biscuit tin and put the lid on tightly. Now the tickets were in a very safe place, and both Mr and Mrs Tick-Tock thought they had been very clever indeed.

Saturday came at last and Mr and Mrs Tick-Tock got ready to go to the circus. They were so excited that they could hardly get dressed. But at last they were ready. They walked out of the front door and locked it behind them.

But before they had reached the end of the road Mr Tick-Tock stopped with a groan.

"We've forgotten the tickets!" he said. "Oh my, we shall have to go back. How silly of us!"

So back they went. The front door was shut, of course, so Mr Tick-Tock felt in his pocket for his key. It wasn't there.

"Have you got the key?" he asked his wife. "Look in your bag."

So she looked – but the key wasn't there either.

"Oh, you are silly!" she scolded her husband. "You really are! Where have you put that key?"

"I haven't put it anywhere," groaned Mr Tick-Tock, turning out his pockets again. "I must have given it to you."

"Well, you didn't," said Mrs Tick-Tock,

almost crying. "Oh dear, don't say we
can't get indoors to find the circus
tickets!"

Mr Tick-Tock stared at his yellow front
door in despair – and then he suddenly
cried out in surprise – for there in the
keyhole was the key! He had left it there
after he had locked the door!

"There's the key!" he cried. "Look!"

"Hurrah!" said Mrs Tick-Tock,
cheering up. "You didn't take it out of
the keyhole. What a good thing we had
to come back for the tickets! Anybody
might have got into the house with the
key in the keyhole!"

Indoors they went. "Now, where did
we put those tickets?" said Mrs Tick-
Tock, looking all round.

"We put them in a very safe place, I
know," said Mr Tick-Tock.

"But where was it?" asked his wife,
frowning hard.

"I know!" cried Mr Tick-Tock, and he
clapped his hands for joy. "I know! It was
in the old biscuit tin!"

"Of course!" said Mrs Tick-Tock. "That

was the safest place we could think of."

So they went to where the biscuit tin stood on the shelf. They lifted it down and took off the lid – and, dear me, what a surprise – it was filled with biscuits. And there were no tickets there at all!

"Look! It's got biscuits in!" said Mr Tick-Tock in surprise. "Have the tickets got covered up?"

He emptied them all out on the table – but there were no red circus tickets there. Mr Tick-Tock looked at his wife.

"Did you put the biscuits there?" he asked, with a frown.

"Yes," said Mrs Tick-Tock. "You see, my sister Jane sent me a pound of oatmeal biscuits as a present, and, of course, I put them in the tin. But I took out the tickets, and I put them somewhere else."

"Then you're a silly, stupid, foolish woman!" said Mr Tick-Tock angrily. "That's just the sort of thing you are always doing. Now I expect you've forgotten where you put the tickets."

"No, I haven't then!" said Mrs Tick-Tock, in a snappy voice. "I remember quite well where I put them! I put them inside the cigarette box, so there!"

They went to the cigarette box and Mr Tick-Tock opened it. It was full of cigarettes – but no tickets were there.

"Well I never!" said Mrs Tick-Tock. "They're gone – and I thought it was such a safe place. Have you put them anywhere, Tick-Tock?"

Mr Tick-Tock went rather red.

"Well, as a matter of fact, now I come to think of it, I did see them there when I went to fill the box with cigarettes," said Mr Tick-Tock. "So I took them out and put them somewhere else."

"Then you are a silly, stupid, foolish man!" said Mrs Tick-Tock angrily. "That's just the sort of thing you're always doing. Now I expect you've forgotten where *you* put the tickets."

"No, I haven't then," said Mr Tick-Tock snappily. "I know quite well where I put them, so there! I put them inside the brown teapot."

Mrs Tick-Tock stared at the brown teapot up on the shelf. Then she took it down and raised the lid to look inside. It was empty.

"Dear me!" said Mr Tick-Tock in surprise. "It's empty. Where can those

tickets have gone? I thought they would be quite safe there. I suppose you haven't moved them, Mrs Tick-Tock?"

Mrs Tick-Tock blushed as red as a tomato.

"That's a funny thing," she said. "I do remember seeing them there now. It was yesterday afternoon, so it was. I took the teapot down to make tea and saw the tickets inside. So I put them somewhere else."

"Then you're a silly, stupid, foolish woman!" said Mr Tick-Tock, in a rage. "That's just the sort of thing you're always doing. Now I expect you've forgotten where you've put the tickets."

Mrs Tick-Tock began to cry.

"You are h-h-horrid to be so c-c-cross!" she wept. "I do know where I put the tickets. I p-p-put them in your shaving-mug so that you would be sure to see them there."

Mr Tick-Tock fetched his shaving-mug and looked into it. There were no tickets there.

"I thought it would be a nice safe

place," sobbed Mrs Tick-Tock. "I don't know where they've gone if they're not there, I'm sure. Have you put them anywhere, Tick-Tock?"

Mr Tick-Tock looked uncomfortable.

"Well, yes, I did put them somewhere," he said. "You see, I saw the tickets in my shaving-mug this morning and I had to take them out before I put my shaving-water in. So I moved them somewhere else."

"Then you're a silly, stupid, foolish man!" cried Mrs Tick-Tock, in a temper. "That's just the sort of thing you're always doing. Now I expect you've forgotten where you've put the tickets."

Mr Tick-Tock frowned crossly.

"Don't you talk to me like that," he said. "Of course I haven't forgotten where I put the tickets. I put them in a very safe place."

"Where was that?" asked Mrs Tick-Tock.

"Inside the clock!" said Mr Tick-Tock, in a proud voice. "What do you think of that for a good place, Mrs Tick-Tock?"

He went to the clock and opened it. He felt at the back, just where the pendulum was swinging – and then he turned round with a pale face.

"They're gone!" he said. "They're not there. Oh my, and I thought they would be quite safe there. Mrs Tick-Tock, don't tell me you've taken them out of the clock!"

"Well, I did, you silly creature!" cried Mrs Tick-Tock. "The tickets pressed on the pendulum and stopped the clock. When I went to see what was the matter I found the tickets there. So I took them out, of course."

"Then you're a silly, stupid, foolish woman!" cried Mr Tick-Tock, in a very cross voice. "That's just the sort of thing you're always doing. Now I expect you've forgotten where you put the tickets."

Mrs Tick-Tock looked at him, ready to cry again. And then suddenly she changed her mind, much to Mr Tick-Tock's surprise, and began to giggle.

"He he-he, he he-he!" she chuckled. "Oh dear! He he-he!"

"Have you gone mad?" said Mr Tick-Tock, staring at his little wife in astonishment. "Don't you know that it is long past time for the circus to start, and we haven't found the tickets yet? Stop laughing, foolish woman, and tell me where you put the tickets when you moved them out of the clock."

"I p-p-p-put them in … p-p-p-put them in y-y-y-your—" giggled Mrs Tick-Tock, and then couldn't say another word for laughing.

"I shall be ANGRY in a minute!" said Mr Tick-Tock, striding up and down the kitchen in a very bad temper. "Stop your silly giggling and tell me where you put those tickets. Then I'll go and fetch them."

"You don't n-n-n-need to f-f-f-fetch them!" giggled Mrs Tick-Tock. "I put them in your overcoat pocket, because I knew you'd wear that to go to the circus, and I thought even if we went out without remembering the tickets it

190

wouldn't matter because they'd be in your coat all the time. Oh dear me – what a joke! There we were halfway to the circus, with the tickets in your pocket all the time and here we have come back all the way home to look for them!"

Mr Tick-Tock put his hand in his overcoat pocket – and there were the two red circus tickets, just as Mrs Tick-Tock had said! He didn't know whether to laugh or cry. At last he decided to laugh with Mrs Tick-Tock, and the two sat

down on kitchen chairs and laughed at themselves till the tears ran down their cheeks.

"It's t-t-t-t-too late to go the c-c-c-circus!" said Mr Tick-Tock at last. "We must go another day – and next time we'll have to buy our tickets, because these are no use now. And we'll ask the ticket-man to keep them for us until we go, and then we shan't need to put them into any wonderful safe places, shall we?"

"That's right," said Mrs Tick-Tock, taking off her coat. "Ah well, we've been very, very foolish, but we'll let it be a lesson to us. We won't be so forgetful again."

But, you know, I rather think they will! Don't you?